THE BAND ROOM

THE BAND ROOM

By

Bob Seay

The Band Room / Bob Seay

ISBN-13: 978-1-0879-5583-4

To my students

Acknowledgments

Thank you to Ginger Seay for believing that I could write a book and insisting that I do so.

Thank you to Phil Belmont, Dr. David Frankel, Perla Chavira, Kaitlyn La Cost, Vanessa Marta, Michael Grudt, Sarah Ausmus, Robin Seay, Ari Martinez and everyone else who held my hand along the way.

Thank you to all my students, former and present day. You have been my teachers.

Finally, thank you to all the people who read my blog at bobseay.com, my Facebook page, and my other online ramblings for your support and encouragement over the years.

Table of Contents

1

Practice Imperfect

He was supposed to be at practice but didn't have the strength, so he decided to sleep in and stay home. When he did decide to go downstairs, she was sitting in the kitchen scrolling her phone, half smiling at pictures of cats or ferrets or baby penguins or whatever came across her screen between sips of coffee, her face framed by the window behind her, a brown silhouette against a gray, rainy sky.

They might as well have been living in separate houses; she had her space, her schedule, her life, and Angel had his. There was apparently some new man in the picture, but Angel had long stopped caring. It wasn't that she dated a lot of men – depending on how you define "a lot" – it was just that Angel no longer really cared what his mother did. He just wanted to make it through his last year of school, graduate, and leave. Get a job as a coach somewhere and live happily ever after.

This wasn't a home. It was a waiting room.

Thunder rumbled in the distance. Heavy raindrops hit the window, randomly at first, the drops still discernible as rhythmic individuals, then more steadily as the individual beats morphed into a single sustained sound. Rain had to be the original white noise.

She glanced upwards. "Was practice canceled?"

"Don't know," said Angel.

Angel wondered why she even asked. Since Dad left, she was a parent only in the strictest biological meaning of the word. She kept scrolling her phone, but her eyes were looking at the rain. "Maybe they're practicing inside today."

"Again – Do. Not. Know."

Angel swung the door to the fridge slowly, back and forth, and searched for nothing in particular. He just didn't want to look in her direction.

Football practice started yesterday. School would begin next week. Angel had gone to Monday's 6:00 AM practice – got to beat the heat – but was present in body only. His mind was on what was coming that afternoon, when a judge who saw him as just another juvenile offender would announce his sentence. He missed yesterday's afternoon practice for quarterbacks and receivers because he was in court. Alone. His mother had to work. He flinched at the thought of having to explain all of this to Coach.

"So you got community service?" she asked, already knowing the answer. She wasn't stupid or oblivious. It was a statement disguised as a question, an unnecessarily passive-aggressive reminder that did not need to be made.

"Ninety hours. I'm supposed to talk to someone at school about what I have to do."

"Any ideas?"

Angel held the fridge door open and drank some grape juice straight from the bottle. It was just one more thing he would not have done when Dad was in the house. But Dad was no longer in the house. His mother didn't drink juice unless it was fermented.

She kept scrolling, intentionally trying not to look at her son. She repeated herself very clearly and much more slowly, her usually slight Spanish accent thickening with the slower tempo of her words. "Angel, do you know what you're going to do for your ninety hours of community service?" Her voice was quiet but persistent, and more than a little agitated. It was the sound of someone who was seeking information but was tired of asking questions.

Ninety hours. The entire court episode was so surreal and so quick that the number didn't sink in right away. It was just a number, a rather large number, but still just another abstract concept. This morning, somehow, it seemed much less abstract.

The most immediate non-abstraction was that this probably meant Angel couldn't play football his senior year. He wasn't sure, but there must be some kind of code of conduct that applied here, some required form of punishment, if for no other reason than to make him an example to other players, the ones who already do the same thing but were yet to be caught in the act. Even if there wasn't some official rule, Angel knew Coach would make his life as miserable as possible. If by some absolute miracle banishment from the team was not required and Coach would let him play, there was still the issue of the ninety hours of slave labor that had to be completed by the end of the semester. He could make the games, but unless he could work this out, he would have to miss the practices after school.

"Angel?" The emphasized second syllable indicated a heightened level of interest in her son's plans.

He put the bottle back in the fridge, glanced at his mother, and went back upstairs without answering her question.

2

Dead Week

After deciding to ghost Coach and the entire football team, Angel had thought he would sleep late and decompress. No reason to get up for a 6:00AM practice now. There was still a week before school started, so no need to get up for that, even though getting to class on time had never been a high priority for Angel. Might as well follow his natural biological clock, stay up late and sleep in.

Instead, he woke up even earlier than the day before. It was as if his body was not aware that his life had changed. On Monday morning, his biggest goal had been to get ready for the final football season of his high school career, then on to play in college. Who knows what might happen after that. Today, his big goal was to find a supervisor for his community service. But his circadian rhythm was stuck at the "get up in time for football practice" setting.

Angel's extreme sleep deprivation was usually by choice and not because he just couldn't sleep, but the video games that usually kept him awake until 1:00 or 2:00 in the morning on most school nights were much less exciting under these circumstances. He was surprised he could still access any games or even the internet at all. He had been sure his mother's contribution to his rehabilitation would be to take his phone and install multiple layers of memory-sucking parental controls on his computer. Surprisingly, neither of those things had happened. He still had his phone and full internet access. Maybe she thought he'd been punished enough, or would be punished enough, or was waiting to see if he had been punished enough. He was sure that the extent of his suffering and misery was a factor here and decided to remember that just in case he needed to act more miserable in the future. Or perhaps she knew he would be too distracted to enjoy any games he might play and had intentionally kept everything open just to punish him even more, taunting him, reminding him of less conscripted times. Or maybe she hadn't thought of any punishment at all. Maybe she just didn't care.

Maybe she'd just given up.

Whatever her plan, it didn't really matter. Angel wasn't playing Overwatch much these days anyway. He wasn't watching stupid videos of people doing stupid things. His community service hadn't even started, and it was already interfering with his life.

Angel's class schedule was already set – more boxes checked off on a template to which he had little meaningful input – so he didn't have to go to registration. He could stay home until the first day of school, doing whatever it is insomniacs call their version of hibernation, but he knew he would eventually have to talk to a counselor. He had one week to find someone – a teacher, a janitor, the school cop, someone at the school – who would serve as his supervisor, to set up a work schedule, and then to get that arrangement approved by the Court. He thought about asking Coach. That would make the most sense. But that would require talking to Coach, and Angel was avoiding that conversation for as long as possible. It had been less than 24 hours since his sentencing, but he was sure Coach already knew at least the outcome if not the details of his situation. And while the jury was still out on how Mom felt about what the judge had done, Angel knew Coach would not be satisfied with *"only"* ninety hours of court-ordered servitude. Whether he was kicked off the team or allowed to stay on as a tackling dummy, Coach would be sure to let him know that Angel owed him even more. Angel could already hear the rant. "You live with your choices! Your personal problems have no bearing on your commitment to this team!" He pictured little drops of spit flying through the air as Coach said, "personal problems."

Whatever. Go team.

3

A Counselor, A Janitor, and a Band Director

Margo Carpenter stared at the list of students with schedule conflicts and wondered how a high school guidance counselor was supposed to put all the rabbits in cages when the rabbits themselves didn't seem to know what they wanted to do or why they should be doing it.

"Why do we bother with spring registration if they're just going to change their mind over the summer?" she asked the kitten hanging by one paw from a branch on a poster on her wall. The poster said, "Hang in there." Beside that was another allegedly motivational poster of an eagle soaring above a tree, captioned with "Soar higher!". Such was the extent of student motivation at Hoag High School. Ms. Carpenter often imagined the eagle snatching the kitten from the tree, the kitten struggling for freedom as the eagle soared over the parking lot on its way to an impromptu lunch date. She vacillated between which of the two best represented her.

Ms. Carpenter was responsible for Junior and Senior schedules, which meant that she not only had to worry about classes at the high school but also had to coordinate with the community college down the street. Several students were on track to graduate from the two-year community college at the same time they graduated from high school.

Angel was not one of those students.

Angel tapped on the open door and spoke quietly. "I need to speak to a counselor."

Ms. Carpenter did not look up to see who was speaking. She pointed to the empty chair facing her desk and drew circles with her finger. "You and half the school. Have a seat."

The desk was covered with stacks of registration forms, folders, and assorted schedule-related ephemera that was urgent for students, but to the counselors were just more forms in an endless cascade of paperwork. The desk was L-shaped, with the long side of the L facing the front door, and two chairs for visitors. The computer was on the short side of the L, to Ms. Carpenter's left, its screen partially obscured by the microphone that Ms. Carpenter used to call students to her office and otherwise interrupt the educational process multiple times each day. There really was no other way to get everything into the small office. The feng shui was as twisted and forced as the exposed roots of the little bonsai tree that claimed most of what was left of the space on her desk. Angel looked at Ms. Carpenter and then started watching the slide show of Ms. Carpenter's cats on her computer screen.

Ms. Carpenter looked up from her paperwork and peered at Angel over the top of her glasses. "What can I do for you?" She wasn't smoking. This was a school, a tobacco-free zone. But it was so easy for Angel to imagine a cigarette in her mouth, bouncing up and down as she spoke, like those movie scenes where some aspiring young actor goes to New York and hires an agent to jumpstart his career.

"I have to do ninety hours of community service. The judge told me to check in with you to get that scheduled."

Angel waited for the long, imaginary stream of cigarette smoke to come from Ms. Carpenter's imaginary cigarette. "Why are you checking in with me?"

"Because that's what the judge said." Angel's voice had more than a touch of condescension, a tone that Ms. Carpenter really did not appreciate and really did not need in her life right now. "He told me to check with the school about my community service."

"Are you sure that's what he said?" Ms. Carpenter leaned her chair back and looked at the student sitting on the other side of her desk. Angel was not the first student to ask her to arrange some court-ordered community service. She did not appreciate the way the courts dropped this part of their job on the schools. If they're going to sentence people to community service, then they should have some system in place to make sure the order was followed. The counselor continued her thought. "Or did he tell you to find someone who would volunteer to help you and to bring your work schedule back to him?"

"Yes. That's what he said. Find someone. So I need to find someone, I guess." He glanced at the computer screen just as the slide-show was changing pictures. Another cat. This cat clearly had attitude.

Ms. Carpenter followed Angel's gaze and looked at the screen to make sure it was a cat and not some confidential student records that had captured Angel's attention. She surveyed the top of her desk and thought about the scheduling conflicts, the independent studies she was going to have to beg teachers to do for students in order to resolve those conflicts, and the inevitably unhappy parents and students who would not appreciate how those conflicts were resolved. Ms. Carpenter thought a lot about conflict. Finding teachers to babysit a juvenile offender was not a battle she wanted to fight.

"The first step in solving a problem is to figure out whose problem it is," the counselor said, as she leaned forward again. She pointed her finger at Angel so she could emphasize each word. "And this sounds like it is your problem." She sat back, pushed her glasses up, and picked up some registration forms.

"So…, you can't help me?"

She did not look up from her forms. "I could help. I am choosing not to." Ms. Carpenter turned to Angel and spread her hands over the paper-covered desktop to illustrate the extent of the problems she had yet to solve. "The second step in solving your problem is for you to visit the teachers or the janitor or someone and see if they would be willing to supervise."

"The second step?" Angel felt that he must have missed something. "What was the first?"

Ms. Carpenter sighed. "Again, the first step in solving a problem is to figure out… " she moved her hand in a circle as she tried to coax a response from Angel.

"Whose problem it is," Angel finished the sentence. "But the judge…"

Ms. Carpenter held up her hand to interrupt. "The judge told you to find someone who would supervise. That is a court order, and you need to do that. Your judge said nothing to me. I have no court order." She paused, then realized the silence probably created a more dramatic effect than she wanted to convey. In reality, she was just considering what to say next. "But you are in luck. The teachers are working in their classrooms today. Is there a teacher you like who might be willing to help?"

Coach was the first name that came to Angel's mind, but that would be way too intense and probably would not happen anyway. If it did happen, there was no telling how many kinds of misery Coach would cram into ninety hours of slave labor. That would not end well. His history teacher was always on him for being consistently late for her first-hour class last semester. He could not expect much sympathy there. And after last year's incident in the chemistry lab, he knew better than to ask anyone in the science department.

"I could ask the janitor, I guess."

"Good idea. He's working today. I suggest you go find him."

Angel wasn't sure which janitor Ms. Carpenter was talking about. There were four that worked in the building, depending on what part of the building and what time of day it was. Angel knew the name of only one of them – Mr. Larch – but that was only because he saw Larch's nametag in what Angel now feared would prove to have been a rather unfortunate first encounter during his sophomore year. This first meeting involved some milk and an unsuspecting freshman boy and ended with Mr. Larch handing Angel a mop and telling him that he could clean up his own mess. That was the extent of their relationship.

A janitor's cart was parked in the hallway near the gym, dangerously close to Coach's office. The gym wasn't the only room in that hallway, but that and the weight room were the only rooms Angel knew. As far as he was concerned, they were the only rooms that mattered. Still, there were other classes in that same direction, the art room, the band room, the weight room, and some other rooms. He wasn't even sure what the other rooms were for. The teachers at this end of the building referred to their area as "the Applied Wing," a subtle jab at the science, math, and English classes in what was called the Academic Wing on the south end of the building. Mr. Larch came out of the gym and started pushing his cart further down the hall.

"Mr. Larch?"

"Yeah?". Mr. Larch turned his head and then his entire body, his slightly stooped shoulders rising as he came around. "Oh. You. Did you pour more milk on another kid?"

So much for a fresh first impression, Angel thought as he caught up to the janitor. "Yeah. I mean, no. Not today. Sorry about that. Can I ask you a favor?"

"OK."

"Is there any work that you need to be done around the school? Anything I could do to help you?"

"I don't hire the help. You need to talk to Mr. Garcia about that." Mr. Garcia was the high school principal. Angel generally avoided conversations or any interaction of any type with Mr. Garcia.

"I'm not looking for a paying job, really. I just wanted to know if you need any help." Angel tried to look as earnest as possible. He felt downright altruistic.

"And you just want to volunteer your services?" The janitor's tone was flat and low. "How community service-oriented of you." Mr. Larch could already tell where this was going – it wasn't the first time a student had come to him with this kind of question – but he thought it would be entertaining to see how Angel would spin it. He was even more interested in how Angel would respond to what he was about to say. He nodded his head towards a door just a few feet away and offered his mop to Angel. "There's a mess in the boy's bathroom that needs to be cleaned up."

Angel backpedaled. "I couldn't start today." He looked at the dirty gray water in the mop bucket. "We would have to work out a schedule."

"So... you need to find someone to help – someone to watch you – and then come up with a schedule." The janitor paused before going on. "Let me guess. Then you have to get the schedule approved, right? Then you have to keep track of how many hours you work?"

"Well, yes. Sir." Angel was not accustomed to saying "Yes sir" to anyone other than Coach, but it seemed appropriate under the circumstances.

"Approved by the court, right?"

"Yes." Angel knew he was defeated. There was no need to say "sir" any more.

"How many hours?"

"Ninety."

"Ninety hours!" The number sounded even larger when said with an exclamation mark. It seemed even worse when Mr. Larch said it again in a much softer tone. "Ninety hours." The janitor shook his head. There was no laugh. Just the rather loud sound of a tired man exhaling.

"What did you do?"

"Well, I was…" Before Angel could answer, a man carrying a tuba as though it was a suitcase stepped into the hallway.

"Hey, Mr. Larch!" The man approached them. Angel knew Mr. Roberts was the music teacher because he had seen him with the band, but that was about it. He wondered why someone would be walking around with a tuba.

Roberts' back-to-school enthusiasm was just a little bit annoying to the janitor. To Mr. Larch, it always seemed that teachers never remembered that janitors work all year. They're on vacation, so they think everyone takes summers off. They're conditioned that way. They've had summers off for how long? Since they were five or six years old? In Paul Roberts' case, that was over fifty years of summer vacations from school. He could see how they could forget how the rest of the world lives.

Mr. Larch ignored the question and nodded his head toward Angel. "Angel here was just asking me if he could help out around the school. Is there anything you need to have done in the band room?"

"I don't think we've met. I'm Paul Roberts." The Band Director reached out with his free arm to shake hands, a move that surprised Angel. *Are there really people who still actually do this?* Angel couldn't remember the last time an adult initiated a handshake that did not involve an award ceremony. Mr. Roberts' grip was firm and sure.

Roberts looked at the obviously athletic young man and wondered why he wasn't at football practice. "You're not a band kid. You're not a choir kid, either. Why is that?" Roberts did not wait for an answer. "Music was your first language. You sang songs before you spoke words.

Ever listened to a baby that's just making sounds? That's a song. Ever listen to a mom talk to her baby?" Roberts did a brief one-man reenactment of a conversation between an infant and her mother. "That's a song. Those are notes. You could write that down and play it on a flute if you wanted to."

"I don't play flute. And I don't sing."

"Yeah." The band director sized up the young man standing in front of him. "You don't strike me as a flute player. But you do sing, or at least you did. You sang before you spoke. Music was your first language."

Mr. Larch had heard the "Music was your first language" speech before. Most of the school had heard it. Or they had at least heard of it. Roberts would stop random students in the hallway between classes, ask them why they weren't in choir, and then launch into his favorite soliloquy before the stunned student had a chance to respond. Angel had somehow missed this monologue until now, probably because he had never been in the Applied Wing for anything other than gym and weights. Or maybe he just didn't look like a singer.

He had never been in the band room.

4

The Band Room

Band rooms have a particular smell even when they're empty. It's a combination of scents, a triad, or maybe even a nice sus chord of fragrances. The bass note is old paper. The rest of the world may be digitized, but music rooms still have dozens of old file cabinets full of aging band and choir music printed on enough yellowing, dusty paper to fill a library. The tenor note, at least in the Hoag High School band room, is the woody, wood-gluey smell of guitars. On alto are old instrument cases, their padded velvet linings slightly musty from being soaked in surprise thunderstorms and football games that should have been called for rain. On top of the chord sits the soprano note, the smell of valve oil, similar to baby oil but not quite. Music students can pick out these smells just like they can pick out the notes of a melody, but for people who haven't spent much time in a band room, they all run together like an elbow smashing down hard on the low end of a piano.

Angel couldn't identify what he was smelling any more than he could have identified the individual notes of a song.

Mr. Roberts straddled a chair and faced backward, rested his arms on the back of the chair, and told Angel to have a seat. Roberts leaned forward towards his guest.

"Talk to me."

"OK. I got into some trouble, so the judge ordered me to do ninety hours of community service. I have to find somewhere to do that."

"And why would you think you could do that in the band room?" Mr. Roberts was not blessed with a naturally friendly face. His default setting was a scowl, which was made worse by a beard that made it difficult to tell when he was smiling. His deep-set blue eyes had the intense gaze of someone trying to look past what's immediately in front of him. As a child, Mr. Roberts heard, "Look me in the eyes!" a lot, usually from his father and typically when he was in trouble. Consequently, his intense eye contact, even in casual conversations, made people think he was angry even when he wasn't. He compensated for his appearance by raising his voice only when it was absolutely necessary or when he was very, very angry. Fortunately, Mr. Roberts only got mad about once a semester. That was usually all it took to make the point.

"Were you ever in band? In Middle School? Beginner band? Anything?"

Angel shook his head and thought about the band geeks he had known in Middle School. *"God. Has my life sunk to this?"*

"Huh." Roberts looked around his room. "Just out of curiosity, what did you do to deserve this opportunity?"

"Well, I..." Angel's voice trailed off. He did not like telling this story.

"Wait," Roberts waved one hand to stop the story. "Doesn't matter. Unless it was for stealing. Did you steal anything?"

"No. I did not steal."

"Murder? Can't really have any murderers in the band room. That could be bad." He stroked his beard thoughtfully. "I mean, the drummers...." His voice trailed off.

Angel couldn't tell if this slightly angry-looking man was serious or not. He shook his head as if to shake off the question, like a boxer shaking off a hard hit to the chin.

"No?" asked Roberts. "Yeah, I would think you would get more than ninety days community service for that." The tone of his voice changed to be consistent with his less intense facial expression. "But, you never know. A good lawyer, some lenient judge. Maybe use the affluenza defense... ". Roberts looked at Angel. Clearly, affluenza did not apply.

Angel did not know how to respond. He had not expected an interrogation, especially not one that bordered on ridiculous. After a few seconds that seemed like forever, Mr. Roberts stood up.

"Honestly, it doesn't matter what you did. You're here now. Let's start with that. I don't usually leave here until 5:30. You could do an hour a day after school for ninety days. That's one semester. Does that work for you?"

Angel answered as he stood up. "What would I be doing?"

"There's always work to do here. You can file music. Or you could file music. If you get tired of that, you can always, I don't know, file music? Are you picking up a theme here?"

Angel looked at the racks of guitars on the other side of the room. "Can I learn to play guitar?"

"Sure. We have a class for that. It's second hour. You can sign up. And then you can come in here after school and file music." Mr. Roberts knew this was not the answer Angel was hoping for, but the flash of hope deteriorating into disappointment was mildly entertaining to watch.

"OK…" Mr. Roberts moved towards the door. "Does that work for you?"

Angel looked around the unfamiliar room and at the strange man at the door. None of his friends were in band or choir. Quite the opposite. It may be cool to be in *a* band. It is not cool to be in *the* Band.

Angel looked at his feet. Then he looked up. "I'll think about it."

"Wow," Mr. Roberts mouthed the word but made no sound. Angel felt like this teacher was trying to look through his eyes and directly into his brain. There was a silent beat before the band director broke his gaze.

"OK. Well, let me know." Mr. Roberts was disappointed, but not surprised. He had not expected Angel to say yes. Mainly he felt like he had wasted his time while this kid tried to get a get out-of-jail-free card. Time was not something Mr. Roberts liked to waste.

Angel left the band room, completely forgetting the room's proximity to the Coach's office. He was looking at his phone when he heard Coach's voice.

"Angel! What happened?"

Coach was standing in the hallway, right in front of his door, just about to go into his room. Another thirty seconds and Angel would have gotten away.

"Sorry, Coach." Angel looked at the floor. "I can't play this year."

"No, you can't. Now, do you want to tell me why?"

"I have to do some things after school."

"So that's it? Just going to quit?" The final syllable hit hard.

"I don't think I have a choice."

"Not anymore, you don't." With that, Coach went into his office and shut the door behind him.

The hall suddenly seemed much, much longer.

5

Mom

For someone with a Master's Degree in Social Work, Delores was at a loss about what to do for her own teenage son. Her Dunning-Kruger confidence had faded with the experience of actually being a parent. In its place was a much greater compassion for the families sent to her office. Delores found herself mentally reviewing cases of families she met before she had a child of her own, noting the gap between academic theory and actual application and hoping she, at the very least, had not done any harm.

Any shred of confidence that may have remained was peeled away with the divorce. More precisely, in the years and increasingly painful months leading up to the divorce. At least that was what she blamed it on. But the more she thought about it, the more she realized it was the marriage that left her damaged. The divorce was the epilogue, an appended chapter just to wrap things up.

What was left was a woman who loved her son and cared deeply about struggling families but felt increasingly inadequate at helping either. In other words, another stressed-out middle-aged Social Worker Mom who's just doing the best she can.

Enter alcohol.

Delores was never a teetotaler, but she didn't drink enough to think of herself as a drinker. Maybe an occasional glass of wine paired with an elegant evening meal with her then-current, now former, husband. Maybe another glass before bed. Since the divorce, the wine had become more frequent, and the meals were definitely much less elegant. She wasn't an addiction counselor – her area of expertise was family counseling – but she knew enough about addiction to know she didn't have a problem. Still, she could see the red flags coming up along the path before her, even if they weren't exactly whipping in the wind. More like the lazy flapping of an occasional gust. Nothing that couldn't be contained.

She didn't see much of Angel these days. When they did happen to be in the same room, they were more like roommates than family. She wasn't sure if this was because of the divorce, her own internal conflicts, or simply because her son was growing up. She had decided it was probably some mixture of all three. In a year, Angel would be on his own and would not need her at all, or so she told herself. She wasn't really sure whether he needed her now. There were days when she felt he would be better off without her.

Angel certainly seemed convinced that he could make it on his own, his current legal complications notwithstanding. But wasn't that the point? To create happy, functional adults who are ready for independent living? Too much of her caseload was the result of parents who failed at that most basic task. But while Angel was undoubtedly independent, Delores wasn't so sure about how happy he was.

Since taking this job, one of her goals as a parent had been to make sure that her son and her family never needed court-ordered counseling.

31

Delores had not even considered the possibility of her son being arrested and sentenced to court-ordered community service.

She poured herself another glass of Bubbly Pink Moscato and nestled back into the couch. Finally relaxed and emotionally exhausted, she eventually fell asleep.

Angel came home a few hours later, his short conversation with Coach still under replay review by the game officials that lived in his head. He saw his mother sleeping on the couch, the empty wineglass resting against her leg, the half-empty bottle on the floor beside her. He found the cork, put it in the bottle, and put the bottle in the fridge. The glass went in the sink. He gently brushed his mother's hair away from her face and watched as the strands fell back to exactly the same position. No sense in brushing it back again. The loose ends didn't seem to bother her, and he didn't want to wake her up.

Then he went upstairs and went to bed.

6

Back to School

Three short pings on the school PA meant that an announcement was about to be made. The ensuing throat clearing and a rather loud "Ahem," followed by a pause before speaking, meant that it was Mr. Garcia on the microphone. The school principal had a habit of forgetting to clear his throat before turning on the microphone. On a good day, it was only borderline disgusting. On a bad day, when Mr. Garcia's allergies were kicking in, and there was a lot of deep hacking sinus draining throat clearing to be heard, it could make you gag. Ms. Carpenter, the only other voice that made frequent appearances on the Hoag High School airwaves, would not make that kind of audible mistake. Or maybe it wasn't a mistake. Perhaps it was Mr. Garcia's way of making sure he had everyone's attention. Like the cocking of a gun.

Mr. Garcia's *basso profundo* voice had the kind of delivery that comes from speaking in large venues with extreme sound delay, like a high school gym or a football stadium. It was like the voice of God. Or a sportscaster.

"Students." Pause as the deep, resonant voice reverberated through the hallways, Darth Vader, minus Vader's contempt for all life forms in the galaxy. "The bells are not working." Another pause. "At this time."

33

Pause. "Please proceed to your first-hour class." Pause. "*This* is your bell." Pause.

"Ding," said the deadpan voice. You could hear the stifled laughter of the office staff just before the mic was turned off.

"Ding," Angel repeated.

This was Angel's twelfth first day of school. There is, of course, only one true First Day of School, just as there is only one First Kiss and only one First Time. For school, it's when your mom drops you off for kindergarten. You're excited, and you think you're going to learn new things. You get to spend the day with a bunch of other kids who are just as excited as you. Everybody's jumping up and down and happy. The First Day of school is a pretty thrilling day for a little kid. Then the system destroys your love of learning while simultaneously crushing any creativity you might have within you. The excitement drops off rather steeply after that.

Angel's first day of his senior year was different only in that it was the first time he felt completely left out of the school's social mix. In keeping with time-honored tradition, the team wore their game jerseys, the dark blue shirts clearly defining who was in and who was out of Hoag High School's most elite social group. Angel was clearly not in this year. The cheerleaders took their cue from the football team and swiveled their collective ponytailed heads away as Angel walked by, their button noses held even higher than usual. None of the other usual tribal clusters – the tribal clusters that Angel had spent the previous three years ignoring – looked especially inviting or even very interesting. He was a Man Without a Clique. He knew his life had hit bottom when he sat at the Pokémon table, and the Pokémon nerds walked away.

Other than the involuntary social distancing, Angel's day went about as he had expected. And as expected, he was late to his second-hour western civ class.

"Angel!" Ms. Bonner called as Angel walked in late. "I see we're picking up right where we left off last year." Angel smiled as he walked to the nearest empty chair and had a seat.

"And could you remove the earbuds?" Bonner didn't miss much.

Angel wanted to ask her about sponsoring his community service. He wasn't really sure exactly what someone could do for ninety hours in a social studies classroom, but he figured it was worth a shot. As class droned on, Angel began to think that his being late on the first day would only make that conversation even more awkward. He decided to arrive early for tomorrow's class and ask then. Then he thought about everything that happens on the first day of school and decided that he might as well not ask any other teachers until later that week. Let things settle. The teachers will be in a better mood.

He was on his way to fifth-hour weights class when he met Roberts in the hallway. Angel had forgotten that the band room was next to the weight room. The band director had two guitar cases in his left hand, and another tucked under his right arm. As he walked, he somehow managed to dig his keys out of his pocket while carrying the single guitar case under the same arm.

"So, you decided not to take guitar class?" Roberts asked. He was way too excited for the first day of school. "We got new guitars!" He lifted the cases towards Angel's face as if he couldn't see them already.

"Yeah. Have to take western civ second hour. Sorry."

"No need to apologize to me. Could you hold this, please? Thanks." Roberts handed the two guitars to Angel and unlocked the band room door. He spoke without looking at Angel. "What about that other thing?"

"Still working on it."

"Be sure you do." Roberts took the guitars from Angel. "Judges have a way of getting upset when they think people aren't taking them seriously." He opened the door.

"Have a day," Mr. Roberts said cheerfully.

"He always says that." Angel looked at the band geek with her big smile and little whatever case. She looked way too excited about getting to class. "He says it's because he doesn't want to set any unrealistic expectations for the day." Clarissa smiled at Mr. Roberts and looked around the band room. "I've missed this room!"

"And the room has missed you," Mr. Roberts smiled at his first chair, two-time All-State Clarinet player who was on track to make it three years in a row. "Welcome back, Clarissa."

Angel walked the short distance to the weight room. He had signed up for the class last year before he was arrested, long before he knew he would not be on the team. It was either weights class or metal shop, and the only "metal" that held any interest for Angel was the sound of the Metal bands that blasted at full volume in the weight room. Had he known how his last year of high school would begin, he would have taken another class. Suddenly welding didn't look so bad. Now, he had to spend one hour a day with Coach. Angel made a mental note to go to the Counselor's office and see if he could change classes.

"Get in here." Coach barely looked at him. His voice was low, like a dog growling before he attacks. "Go get dressed."

And that was all Coach said to him that day. Six words. Coach gave the usual back to school speech to the class, talked about weight lifting, safety, and the rules of the room. Coach was big on rules. But the man who stepped up as a father figure as Angel's parents were going through their divorce had no inside jokes or reassuring words for him today. Angel felt relief and sadness at the same time. The absence of any football players in the class only contributed to Angel's sense of sad relief; sad he was alone, relieved that no one could see his shame. The team lifted before and after school when Coach opened the room and let them in. Weight class was for non-athletes who needed another PE credit but didn't want to spend a semester playing badminton or running around the gym for an hour. Angel was only there because there was no place else to be. He watched an especially skinny boy struggle to balance an empty barbell on the bench press. Probably a Pokémon nerd. These people definitely were not athletes. Angel had thought this would be a nice break in the afternoon. Now he wasn't so sure.

And that was Angel's first day. And his second, if you take away the conversation with Mr. Roberts and the passing glance from Coach. And his third, which included passing eye contact with Roberts in the hallway but no words. Rinse and repeat. Coach was still not speaking to him, which was awkward but, Angel thought, much better than the alternative. At least there was a routine. In fact, everything was so routine that Angel was surprised when an unexpected text message showed up as he was going to fourth-hour biology II with Ms. Coats.

Case 246-01: This is a courtesy reminder that the deadline for filing your Community Service Agreement with the Court is 5:00 tomorrow afternoon. Failure to do so may result in a bench warrant for your arrest and other penalties. All agreements are subject to Court approval.

"Great."

Angel stepped into the classroom and sat down. What could he do for ninety hours? What would the judge approve? He thought about pretending he didn't get the message, but he knew this wasn't going to go away.

"None of this would have happened if I hadn't crossed that street," he thought. It really was a case of just being in the wrong place at the wrong time. He was going to get a haircut when he saw a crowd across the street. A large and very angry man with a megaphone was on the steps of the courthouse. Angel could hear him but could not make out what he was saying, only that he was angry and very forceful. He crossed the street to see what was going on. The crowd was encouraging the man with the microphone, shouting "Yes!" and "No!" and other things in response to what the man was saying. Each response was louder than the one before.

The police that had been standing on the crowd's edge inched closer, their semi-circle formation growing tighter with each step until they eventually blocked Angel's view.

Angel was moving towards the line of dark blue shirts when he tripped and fell, striking one officer in the back with his elbow, right between the officer's shoulder blades. The officers were not expecting someone to come up from behind. Angel tried to break his fall by grabbing a surprisingly hard and well-muscled arm. That arm then put Angel on the ground with more force than he had ever experienced in three years of high school football.

"NO!" the voice barked. Angel tried to get up. "Stay down!".

Another cop spun around. "You just assaulted a police officer!"

"No. No. I was just..."

"Get up!" Angel's body was pulled from the ground, and his arm nearly pulled out of its socket. Angel felt hands going up and down his body. He was being frisked. "What's in there? Empty your pockets!"

Without thinking, without speaking, Angel did as he was told.

"Is that...?" He glared at Angel. "You have got to be kidding me." The two officers looked at each other, then both looked at Angel. Officer Big Biceps spoke. "Is this weed? I hope you're high right now because I do not want to think that you are seriously stupid enough to bring weed to a Black Lives Matter protest."

"I'm not high. And I'm not protesting." Angel winced from the sharp pain in his shoulder. "I just wanted to see what was going on." Angel wasn't lying. He wasn't high. If he had been high, he probably wouldn't have been distracted by the crowd. He definitely would not have walked up to a line of cops. *"Great,"* he thought. *"I'm going to go to jail because I wasn't high."* The irony was funny, but this was not the time to laugh.

"So, you're just stupid?" And that's why you have two buds and a pipe in your pocket?" He shoved the incriminating evidence in Angel's face. "Was *this* so you could see what's going on?" The officer was not laughing. He wasn't even smiling. No one in Angel's world smiled that day.

39

Angel relived the rest of the day as he ignored the lecture in biology class. Just the wrong place at the wrong time. The wrong day to have anything in his pockets. The wrong day to get out of bed. Just the wrong day all the way around.

He stopped by the band room on his way to weights.

Mr. Roberts was standing in the hallway by the door, his favorite Fender bass hanging on its strap at his side, making his "music was your first language" speech for anyone who paused long enough to hear. "You can still change your schedule! It's not too late!" He waved the bass like a street preacher waves a Bible. The Gospel According to Paul Roberts.

Angel stepped up and spoke in almost a whisper. "Can we talk about that thing?"

"I can't talk right now. The bell's about to ring. You need to get to class."

Roberts stepped into the band room and watched as students put their instruments together and took their seats. He passed Clarissa as he walked to the podium.

"You could have talked to him," she said as she put her clarinet together. "We can do scales without you."

"I know what he needs. He has to decide if he really wants it. We'll talk then."

40

7

The Offer

If the smell of a band room could be compared to a nice sounding musical chord, then the sound of a band room after school when students are practicing on their own is a hot steaming mess. Angel noticed that sound as he walked down the hall: clarinets, trumpets, drums, a sound he could not identify. More sounds he could not identify. Was that an electric guitar? And what was *that?* He could not sort out what he was hearing. It was as random as it was loud. And it was extremely loud.

The volume increased by a factor of at least seven when Angel opened the door. Students were scattered around the room, a few in pairs but mostly alone, working on everything from scales to songs that Angel could almost recognize. A trumpet player was trying and failing to hit high notes. A drummer was practicing fills. Again and again and again. The bass player was setting up his amp. In the middle of all of this – literally sitting on a stool in the middle of the room – was Mr. Roberts, playing a simple brown classical guitar as if there was no other sound in the world.

Angel walked up. "Can I talk to you? I need to talk to you."

"You do?" Roberts looked up without moving his head. He had one ear close to the guitar and the other aimed at the ceiling, his left hand carefully turning a tuning peg. The band director strummed an E chord. Once his sense of pitch was satisfied, he stood the guitar on the floor. The guitar stood straight up, not on its side, but straight up, like a short, brown person with big hips and a long neck. Roberts pulled his hand away slowly after balancing the guitar on its bottom. "Stay, Fred."

"Fred?"

Clarissa walked past, clarinet in hand. "The guitar's name is Fred," she said without breaking her stride or looking at either of them. "I'm going to the stage."

Roberts looked at Fred with genuine affection. "Fred is 38 years old." He picked up the guitar and returned it to playing position, then embraced the instrument like a beloved pet, his face resting against the headstock. If the guitar were a dog, it would have licked him and wagged its tail.

Roberts saw the awkward expression on his visitor's face.

"What's up? Let me put Fred away." He got up and carefully placed the guitar on a stand beside his podium. "Let's go to the stage. Easier to hear."

The band room and the auditorium were connected by a short hallway that went from the band room directly to the backstage area behind the curtains. The passageway made it easier to move instruments and people to the stage for concerts and other performances. But mostly the stage was used as a quiet place for private conversations or a place for very serious musicians to practice when the band room was just too loud and too random even for them. Clarissa, the most serious music student

42

at Hoag High School, was practicing her clarinet on the other side of the stage when Angel and Roberts walked on. Angel knew nothing about playing clarinet, but he knew enough about dexterity to know that Clarissa must be really good to play that fast.

"What's up?" Mr. Roberts pronounced the phrase as one quick word.

"I was wondering if you still needed someone to work after school?"

"Oh. I didn't realize this was about my needs."

Awkward silence.

"I was wondering if I could do my community service in the band room after school?"

Clarissa stopped playing her clarinet and suddenly seemed very interested in adjusting the reed on her instrument. Roberts noticed the silence. He side-eyed Clarissa. She looked right back at him and began a chromatic scale starting on the absolute lowest note of the clarinet. Her command performance was very slow and played with great deliberation, with an accented crescendo on each note.

Roberts looked back at Angel. "You know what the job is. Are you still interested?"

Angel wanted to say, "I'm running out of options" or "I don't really have a choice" or "Is it always that loud?". Instead, he simply said, "I do."

Roberts flinched. "Be careful with that phrase." The band director stepped back towards the door to the band room. "Would you like to see the music library before you sign on for this?"

Angel followed him into the room.

The band room was still just as loud and just as random. Roberts opened the door to the place where the file cabinets were kept. "Here we are."

The room looked like it had survived a storm. Or maybe there were no survivors. Pieces of sheet music were everywhere. Aging manila folders sat on top of file cabinets in stacks and piles that were several feet high. The file cabinets themselves sat in two rows of 12 file cabinets each. The rows faced inward, with an aisle that could not have been more than about four feet between them. A table in the middle of the already narrow aisle held more stacks, mostly of loose sheets of unsorted parts of songs. A countertop at the end of the room farthest from the door was also stacked with music. Angel felt surrounded.

Angel was so overwhelmed by the debris field that he hardly noticed his phone vibrating in his pocket. He was still taking in all the destruction when he felt his phone buzz a second time. Without thinking, Angel took his phone from his pocket and looked at the missed call. "BLOCKED NUMBER," it said. "Uggh," Angel groaned. "I hate phone spammers." Without really noticing, he put the phone on top of one of the stacks of paper.

Roberts looked around the room as if he was experiencing the cataclysm for the first time. It was the shock that comes when you see your world through new eyes, the eyes of someone who has never seen this before. "Another student was in the process of reorganizing this, but she didn't finish," he said quietly. Roberts was embarrassed by the condition of the file room, but it was a shame he had learned to bear. This mess was not from reorganizing the library. The library was being reorganized because it was a mess.

"I probably should have come in and worked on this over the summer." Roberts' voice trailed off as he mindlessly moved loose sheets of music to another, slightly shorter stack of loose sheets of music which, in turn, tumbled over and scattered on the table before cascading to the floor. Roberts shook his head and pointed to the door. "Let's go back to the stage."

Clarissa was taking her clarinet apart and putting it away, a ritual that seemed to slow down as Roberts and Angel came into view.

"Are you sure you want to do this?" Mr. Roberts' voice had the tone of someone about to push a beginning parachute jumper out of a plane.

Angel considered his options, or, more precisely, his lack of options, and the possible consequences of not meeting his deadline. "Yes."

"OK. I've done these things before. You get everything approved by the Court. We'll start then."

"Thank you." It was all Angel could think to say.

Clarissa had kept her distance while Angel was in the room. She approached Roberts as Angel left. The student and teacher went back to the band room together.

Roberts looked at the clock. It was almost 5:00, not as late as he usually stayed. It just seemed later for some reason. He looked around the room and waved one hand over his head. The sound tapered to a stop.

"Thank you for practicing. I hate to say it, but I need to go." Instruments went into cases, cases went into lockers, and students made their way towards the door. Roberts said goodbye to each student as they left the room.

8

Hopes and Expectations

Clarissa stayed around while Roberts put the guitars away. "Is that kid going to work in the library?"

"That is the plan." Roberts straightened the choir music stacked on the piano that doubled as his desk in the band room. "And that kid's name is Angel."

"OK. Do you expect *Angel* to do..." She stopped talking and pointed her finger to the library. "That place?"

He smiled at Clarissa. "I have no expectations."

"You've said that before."

"Because it's true."

"That just seems sad to me."

Roberts looked at her. "Why?"

"Because without expectations, there is no hope."

"Really?" He shook his head. "Because I don't think I said that I have no hope. I am very hopeful that that kid, as you so eloquently called him, will bring structure to my admittedly somewhat chaotic world. Or that he'll just get the music off the floor so I can find what I need in there. I hope for a lot of things. I just don't expect any of them to happen."

"And that isn't sad?" asked Clarissa.

Angel stuck his head in the door before Roberts could answer Clarissa's question. He seemed mildly panicked, on the verge of being moderately upset. "Sorry. Have you seen my phone? I think I left it in here."

Roberts and Clarissa shook their heads. "Haven't seen it," Roberts said, glancing around the room. "Wait. We were in the library. Look in there."

Roberts looked back to Clarissa. "How is that sad? I said I have hope. How can you be sad when you have hope?" Mr. Roberts sat down on the piano bench. "I just have no delusions about how people act or what people will or will not do." Roberts looked straight at Clarissa.

"Delusion brings disappointment. I didn't give up hope. I gave up delusions. I stopped holding people to my unrealistic expectations. And I am happier."

From the library, they heard the sound of an avalanche of sheet music cascading to the floor. It was followed quickly by a muffled but deep groan of frustration. Roberts grimaced at the thought of even more papers scattered across the floor.

Clarissa saw his reaction. "Like the delusion that he will find his phone in there?"

"Yes." Roberts looked towards the library, thinking of what was inside. "That specific delusion will probably lead to great disappointment."

He walked to the whiteboard, picked up a marker, and drew a big plus sign. "So, we'll call this axis Hope and this axis Expectations." He wrote the words on their corresponding axis and pointed to the upper left-hand corner of the crudely drawn graph. "This is High Expectations and Low Hope. Constant disappointment. Just a frustrating place to be." He stepped back a little to look at the whiteboard. "These people…" he pointed to the High Expectations, Low Hope quadrant, "these people should probably avoid open windows when they're upstairs."

"Found it!!!" Angel emerged victorious, phone in hand, and looking like he had just scored a game-winning touchdown.

"Congratulations!" Roberts beamed an *"I told you so"* smile at Clarissa and gestured with both hands. "See? He's happy because he had low expectations but high hope. Just like me." Roberts smiled at how such a convenient example just happened to be right there when he needed it.

Angel wasn't sure what he had walked in on. Something about avoiding open windows. He stopped by the door and looked back to see what Roberts had written on the whiteboard. Roberts noticed that Angel was listening.

"I was saying that people with unrealistic expectations and very little hope should probably avoid open windows." Roberts moved his hand across the graph, to the high expectations and high hope, upper right-hand corner of the graph. "These people often have unrealistic expectations, *and* they are overly optimistic about reaching their unrealistic goals. This was me my first few years of teaching."

Clarissa looked at Roberts. "Honestly, that still sounds like you when we start selling band candy every year. Overly optimistic about unrealistic expectations."

Angel looked at Clarissa. "Coach is the same way. I hate fundraising."

"Fair enough." Roberts drew little dollar signs in the High Expectations, High Hope quadrant as he spoke. "But you can see why people in sales would be here. They almost have to be that way to survive. They need expectations to keep them going and hope to motivate them when they can't sell enough candy bars. Or life insurance. Clicky ballpoint pens. Whatever."

"But even for those of us who don't live to sell band candy, this is still a tricky corner. It can be a good place if it keeps you motivated like it does those sales guys, but even if you reach your goal, you might still think it's not a big deal because you were expected to be there. Or someone else expected you to be there, so they don't think it's a big deal. They're wrong, by the way. And so are you, if you think accomplishing something that you set out to do is no big deal. It's a big deal any time someone reaches a goal they set for themselves, even if, on some days, it's just having the strength and courage to get out of bed."

Clarissa took the marker from Roberts and drew a clarinet in the same box. "The first time I made All-State, I had high hopes and low expectations. I was really happy when I made it, even if I was near the bottom of the section."

Roberts nodded towards Clarissa while he looked at Angel. "You have a lot better chance of getting what you hope for when you do the work."

Clarissa looked back to the whiteboard. "I didn't even expect to make the band. That's how off the chart low my expectations were. The second time I tried out, I had higher hopes and higher expectations. So I was," she pointed to the high hope, high expectation square, "Right here." She looked at Roberts. "And even though I expected to make it, I was still happy when it happened."

Roberts remembered that year, too. "True. But you didn't expect to make third chair. So, in a way, your hope was still higher than your expectations." He took his marker back from Clarissa. "You were happy because you did not expect to get third chair." Roberts loved to brag about his superstar clarinet player. "Clarissa is, by definition, the third-best clarinet player in the state right now. She did *that* as a junior."

Clarissa wasn't satisfied with being the third best. "I wanted first."

"I know. I was there." Roberts reminded her. "But you didn't expect to get first. I remember you saying you would be happy just to be on first clarinet part, which is what? The top six chairs? You made third chair. That's why you were happy."

Angel looked at Clarissa. "So, the goal is first chair this year?"

"That would be nice."

"At this point, you and I both expect you to make the band. I don't think that is unrealistic." Roberts looked at Angel. "She's not being cocky. It's just that she's shown she can make it. It's still a big deal – a very big deal – to make it at all, but Clarissa's at a whole other level than she was two years ago. She's had to adjust her expectations to match her ability. And she keeps on working to make sure she keeps getting better."

Clarissa nodded. "Right."

He pointed his marker to the square with Clarissa's clarinet in it. "A lot of these people are never satisfied. It can be motivating, but it can also be frustrating. And they can get depressed if they start to feel like no matter what they've accomplished, they should have done more." He warned Clarissa. "You have to avoid that trap. Remember to give yourself credit for what you accomplish."

Clarissa had a huge smile as she explained her plan to Roberts. "I'm not just auditioning for All-State this year. I mean, I am, but my main goal is to get a full-ride music scholarship." She turned towards Angel. "All-State players get all kinds of scholarship offers. I've been getting them for two years now. The better you do, the more the scholarship. This year's audition isn't just about getting first chair. This is how I'm going to pay for college."

Angel understood. "That could be very motivating."

"And very rewarding," she said. "Like, literally, *very* rewarding."

Angel knew there was more to this than what Roberts was saying. "We had high expectations and high hopes of winning the state championship last year. Coach was really mad when we lost."

Roberts nodded. "That happens. Especially if you're really attached to the idea of winning. The higher your expectation, the stronger that attachment, the greater the fall if you don't make it. If your identity is based on you winning a contest, then what happens to that identity when you don't win?"

Angel took a couple of steps towards the whiteboard. Roberts pointed to the lower-left corner of his graph. "This block is Low Expectations and Low Hope. These people are defeated before they start if they even start at all. This is the sad corner. Too many people are stuck here."

Angel thought about his own ratio of expectations to disappointments lately. He could see how he was rapidly approaching the corner of the Low Expectations, Low Hope space.

Roberts pointed the marker at Clarissa. "Do you see where I'm going with this?"

He pointed to the lower right-hand corner. "This is Low Expectations and High Hope. This is me." He tapped the whiteboard with the market to emphasize the point, leaving several little freckled dots on the graph in the process. "I hope people do what's right. I hope they do well." He looked directly at Clarissa. "Just like I hope all people will be kind to one another. And I hope for world peace. And the creation of some kind of string cheese that isn't mozzarella." He pointed to Angel. "I *hope* Angel here can perform a miracle in the library. But I have no delusions that any of those things will happen."

Roberts stepped back from the whiteboard. "Delusion brings disappointment."

Clarissa looked at the graph and wondered what her coordinates would be about most of the things in her life. "Yeah. You mentioned that already."

Roberts admired his graphing skills. "I am here." He drew an X right in the middle of the Low Expectations, High Hope quadrant. "I am rarely disappointed and often pleasantly surprised."

Angel looked at the points on the graph. "Coach would say that having low expectations means that you've just given up."

Roberts shook his head. "You're confusing expectations with the ability to recognize potential. My expectations have nothing to do with what I think of someone's potential. I see potential all the time. I teach smart, incredibly talented people with all kinds of potential for all sorts of things. And everyone has the potential to be a decent human being. But that's all it is most of the time. Potential. Unrealized potential. Promising, but not yet realized."

The band director shook his head. "Again. Delusion, magical thinking, all of that just brings disappointment."

Roberts looked back at the whiteboard graph. "I push my students to be the best they can be. That is my job." He looked at Angel, then at Clarissa. "I love my job. But I had to quit feeling disappointed when some of them would not reach my expectations. Maybe there was something else going on in their life that I didn't even know about, something that really kept them from accomplishing what they wanted to accomplish, something they could have accomplished under different circumstances. And maybe my expectations, under those circumstances, were just unrealistic.

Roberts walked towards the piano. "I finally learned that most people are just doing the best they can." He sat on the piano bench and said nothing more.

Angel broke the silence. "OK. Well. Yeah. I'll get this turned in, and I guess I'll see you Monday."

"See you Monday."

Roberts waited for Angel to leave. "Do you know that guy?"

"Kind of. I mean, he's a senior. We've had some classes together, but I don't really know him. He's a football player, but I've heard he's not playing this year. I don't know why. I can't imagine being in band all through high school and then not doing band my senior year. I don't know why you would be on the football team for three years and then quit your last year. Especially someone like that. He's like Mr. Football."

"What's he like?"

"I think I just said, 'he's like Mr. Football.'"

"Uh-huh." *What is it about high school seniors that gives them that naturally sarcastic sound?*

Clarissa continued. "I have no idea. I mean, he's been in some of my classes, but I never really got to know him. He doesn't really talk to anyone who doesn't play sports. And I'm not a cheerleader, so I'm not even on his radar. I don't think he's a great student. He doesn't cause trouble, but he doesn't really do much in classes either." Clarissa paused and thought for a moment. "I really don't know him very well at all. Why was he even in here?"

"He needed to talk to me."

"So, I gathered."

Clarissa looked at the graph on the whiteboard. She'd seen this before. "Do you have low expectations for me?" She smiled as if to say, "Gotcha!"

"I have low expectations for humanity, Clarissa. You…" he stopped walking and looked to watch Clarissa's reaction to what he was about to say.

"You are not human. You're a musician."

9

Court Dates and Lunch Breaks

Angel was supposed to be at school but didn't have the focus, so he decided to stay home. There was no point in even trying to sleep in. He still wasn't sleeping much these days. When he finally decided to go downstairs, she was sitting at the kitchen table looking out the window.

"No school today?" Another question to which she already knew the answer.

"Not going. Court." He opened the refrigerator door.

"Oh. Yeah." She raised her coffee mug to her lips and held it there for a few seconds before she finally took a sip. "That." She put down the mug but did not look at her son. "Do I need to be there?"

"I wouldn't know why." His blunt reply hurt just a little, just one more reminder of her fading importance in her son's life. "I'm supposed to be there at 10:00. I'll go to school after that. Shouldn't be a big deal."

"OK." She put the mug in the sink and went to her bedroom to get ready for work. "Love you."

No response.

As Delores dressed for work, she thought about what she would say to a family if a family like hers showed up in her office. Her first thought was that a family like hers would not be in her office. There was no abuse here, no troubled souls, no crisis she couldn't handle. There was distancing, the healthy distancing that occurs between a young adult and a parent. Still, she couldn't remember the last time she heard her son call her "Mom." It was usually just "Hey," followed by whatever it was he had to say, which seemed to be less and less lately. Angel didn't really answer her questions or even respond to any attempts she made at conversation, but, again, that's not unusual for a 17-year-old boy. That kind of thing seemed pretty normal, based on the 17-year-olds she had seen in her office. Then again, those 17-year-olds *were* in her office, more under court order than not. Perhaps her statistical sample was a bit skewed. Her perception of what a typical family should look like might be a bit off by now. But it was certainly not the kind of thing that caused a family to seek counseling, court-ordered or otherwise.

Once again, there were red flags, but they weren't waving in the wind. She decided it was nothing she couldn't handle. She thought about all of this as she took a sip from the bottle she kept in her dresser, a little Moscato for the morning.

Then she left for work.

Angel turned in his paperwork at the courthouse at the duly appointed time. He wasn't sure what he had expected, but it all seemed very procedural and anticlimactic. He didn't even see the judge. The woman at the counter looked over the forms to make sure everything was signed and filled out. She disappeared into some other room. Then she came back. "Be sure and get this done by the end of the year. This year. Not the school year. Do not forget."

"Thank you. I will." And that was it. The whole thing took about fifteen minutes, less time than it had taken for him to drive to the courthouse. Angel had expected more drama, more pressure. Just... more. He wasn't sure if what he felt was disappointment or relief. He was familiar with disappointment. He was not as familiar with relief.

He thought about going to his mother's office since he was already close by, but why? To tell her something that she didn't really care about? The more he thought about that little family reunion, the less he wanted to make a surprise appearance. Besides, she was probably in a meeting.

He thought about going to school. He told the attendance office that he would be in court today. The secretary insisted on seeing his paperwork. As if someone would lie about something like that. "*Although*," he thought, "*being in court would make a great excuse for missing class.*" And he was already marked as absent. Even better, he was already marked "excused" absence. The paperwork that the secretary saw only showed his court order and that he would be working with Mr. Roberts. It did not specify when he was supposed to be in court or when he would be free to leave. It wasn't even 10:30 yet. He could skip at least until after lunch, maybe even the entire day.

As he left the courthouse parking lot, he drove past the spot where what he now referred to as "the incident" occurred. "*Just in the wrong place at the wrong time,*" he thought. He rubbed his hand against the empty front pocket of his jeans. At least he hadn't needed to worry about dropping *those* items in the little tray beside the metal detector. He hadn't smoked since the arrest. The same court order that required him to do ninety hours also required him to take a drug class and to be subject to random drug testing. He assumed that part of this ordeal would be starting soon now that his community service had been set up. Great. One more thing to look forward to.

Surely they wouldn't check today…

No. Angel dismissed the thought of any herbal recreation, at least for now, before his ninety hours of community service became ninety days in his community's jail or whatever the going rate is for that kind of thing. Still, there was no need to rush back to school, certainly not before lunch. The bell for 5th Hour didn't ring until 12:18. Might as well go home, get in some game time before lunch, and then go back.

The more Angel thought about it, the more impressed he was with himself and his recent good behavior. He probably would not have chosen this path to sobriety, but he hadn't smoked since the night before "the incident." He had not only shown up for all of his court appearances, he had also shown up on time. That alone was a significant accomplishment. He arranged the entire community service thing on his own even though Ms. Carpenter had been absolutely no help at all. Surely he deserved a reward. Some special treat.

It was coming up on 11:00. That Thai place that he liked opened at eleven. It's early enough that there shouldn't be a crowd. He decided to take himself out for lunch. A couple of traffic lights and a few left turns, and he was there.

As Angel expected, the place was almost empty. The waiter pointed to a table and told him to have a seat. There was no need for Angel to get a menu. He knew what he wanted. "Pad Thai, very spicy." His usual order.

"How many stars?"

"A galaxy."

The waitress went to the kitchen. Angel imagined the cook strapping on a gas mask before ladling on the chili oil and those really hot little red Asian peppers.

Angel scrolled his phone and occasionally glanced up to see if his order or at least his drink was on the way. He noticed a couple in the back corner of the room. The man was facing Angel. His face looked just a little older than him. This guy was laughing just a little too loud for Angel's taste. Both the man and the woman seemed really engaged in the conversation. Their heads moved back and forth in some strangely choreographed dance like they were sharing some conspiratorial but hilarious secrets. Angel didn't know this guy. But that... That was clearly the back of his mother's head. And he thought he recognized what she was wearing. Then he heard her laugh and he knew.

"Huh." Angel tried to scrutinize without seeming to stare. *Isn't this guy too young for her? Seriously. What is he? Early 20s? Maybe?*

Then it dawned on him. "Wow. My mother is a cougar," he said to no one at all. As if on cue, the waiter arrived with his drink. Angel just kept staring straight ahead. "Thank you." Angel's voice was barely loud enough for the waiter to hear. "Can I just get my food in a box to go?"

He watched his mother and hoped she wouldn't turn around and see him. When did she start drinking beer? When did she start drinking beer for lunch in the middle of a workday? And when did she meet this guy?

Angel watched the waitress walk back to their table. He thought about leaving before his mother turned around, but then he thought, *"Why should I?"* and decided to stay. Angel caught a glimpse of the side of her face as she talked to the waitress. She wasn't speaking loudly, but he knew her voice. *"She's going to see me,"* he thought. But she didn't. She looked at whoever this guy was, Mr. Choreography. Mr. Smiling and Weaving Like a Damn Cobra. Mr. Cougar Hunter. The waitress left and then returned to their table with two more beers.

After one of those times when time seems to stop, the waitress brought Angel's lunch in all its extra spicy generic white Styrofoam glory. Angel paid and exited as quickly and quietly as possible. He thought about what he had seen as he drove home. That was apparently the new boyfriend, or whatever old people call the people they date. The beer was funny. He laughed to himself about how he caught her doing something wrong for a change. Should he tell her he was there? "No," he decided. Better just to let this go.

Angel checked his phone. Still enough time to go home and eat. It was Friday. The first football game would be tonight, but it was out of town. He wasn't sure if he would have gone if he had been here anyway. He sure wasn't going to drive to wherever it was to watch someone else playing the position that should have been his. Would have been his.

Was no longer his.

He wished he had a friend to call, but all of his friends were either on the team or connected to the team. They would be at the game. And it was becoming clear that the guys on the team were not the kind of friends who rushed to your side in your time of need anyway. That was disappointing. He could have used a friend through some of this. Was that expecting too much?

It was depressing. Still, he managed to be on time for fourth-hour biology. Early even. He took his seat, put in his earbuds, and wondered if she'd gotten the sticky orange chicken that she always got back when they went to their favorite place together.

10

Empty Nest

Angel spent most of the rest of the day wondering what was going on with his cougar mother. His distraction was rewarded by Coach speaking to him for the first time since school began.

"Hey! Angel!" Coach yelled and pointed to the bench press. "Watch what you're doing before somebody gets hurt!" Angel was standing behind the bench press, spotting for this skinny kid who wasn't going to make the lift and may or may not have realized he was about to crush his trachea. Angel snatched the barbell and curled it to his chest.

Skinny Kid sat up, gasping for air. "Thank you!"

"Sorry, man. I really thought you were going to make it," Angel lied. He wouldn't even have known this kid was in trouble if Coach hadn't yelled at him. Coach shook his head and walked further away.

Angel looked around the room to see what else he hadn't noticed. That weird kid over there, the one who was trying to do curls with a dumbbell and laughing about it, looked familiar, but Angel couldn't say from where. Same with the other laughing kid standing there. They did not look like they belonged in a weight room or had ever been in a weight room before. They were taking turns curling a 10-pound dumbbell and laughing about who could make the most grimacing face while doing so. Then Angel remembered where he had seen them. The band room. They were in there practicing in all that noise. *"So this is how band geeks look outside of their natural habitat,"* Angel thought. He wondered if Mr. Choreography had been a band geek. He decided probably not. He was too smooth for that.

The band geeks he was currently watching in the weight room were trying different poses they had seen in some ad for gym clothes for people who think gym clothes are a fashion statement. He guessed they didn't realize the 50-pound barbells in those ads were fake and didn't actually weigh much more than the 10-pound dumbbell they were lifting.

Hashim and Skyler noticed Angel looking in their direction. "Why is he staring at us?" Skyler did not like it when people stared.

"Because you're beautiful," Hashim said.

"Right." Skyler giggled. "Because I'm beautiful." Skyler curled the incredibly heavy 10-pound dumbbell and tried to maintain a weight lifter's scowl before losing it and laughing again.

"Does he know us?" Hashim asked. He looked at Angel again, then at Skyler. "He looks like he knows us." They both giggled again.

Skyler put the dumbbell down. "I don't know him. Just another guy who stares." Eye roll. Hair flip. More giggles.

The bell rang. Angel thought he would stop by the band room and tell Mr. Roberts he could start on Monday.

"Good to know. I'll see you then." Roberts looked past Angel to the door where Hashim and Skyler were standing as if they were waiting for permission to enter. He didn't know why they were standing there. This was their band room. They didn't need permission to come in. "Hashim, could you and Skyler pack up these drums for the game tonight?"

"Sure," Skyler said. She pointed to the music library, where the file cabinets full of sheet music and all the music for band and choir was kept. "Can I go in here first to change out of this?" Skyler was still dressed in gym clothes. She stopped as she was going through the door to the music library. "Can we just make this a regular thing? Me changing in here after weights every day? That would make my life so much less complicated."

"Absolutely," was Roberts' immediate response.

"Thank you!!!"

Roberts turned to Hashim. "You want to stand by and make sure no one walks in there?"

"Was planning on it."

Angel wondered why Skyler couldn't just change in the locker room like everybody else but thought he probably shouldn't ask. *"Must be a religious thing,"* he thought. *"Maybe she's just shy."*

Roberts looked back at Angel. "Anyway. Yes. I'm glad that's all approved and ready to go. Have a weekend. I'll see you Monday."

"Sure. Have a weekend." Angel laughed just a little when he remembered what that girl said about Roberts not wanting to give anyone unrealistic expectations of having a good time.

Hashim waited until Angel was gone to say anything. "That guy was staring at Skyler in weights."

Mr. Roberts thought he knew why Angel might stare, but he wanted to hear how Hashim would explain it. "Why would he stare at Skyler?"

Skyler emerged from the library in a skirt and blouse, looking much more feminine than she had in the weight room. Skyler and Hashim looked at each other and snickered. "I told Skyler it's because she's beautiful." Hashim cocked an appraising eye towards Skyler. "Your eyeliner does look good today, by the way."

"Thank you."

"Really. It really does."

Skyler laughed and batted Hashim's hand away from her face.

Mr. Roberts smiled at his freshman drummer and his sophomore bass player as they put drums in cases and got things ready to go for the game. "Yeah," he said. "It was your eyeliner. We'll go with that." Skyler laughed and flipped her hair. It was good to hear Skyler laugh.

Angel managed to be slightly less distracted for his marketing class sixth hour. Between thinking about his cougar mother and wondering about that kid in weights, he managed to catch most of what Mr. Hernandez said. Something about how in marketing, you list the benefits of a product first and then talk about its features. Benefits are apparently exciting. Features are apparently not as sexy. Or maybe it was the other way around. Maybe you could have really sexy features, but the benefits just weren't that exciting. He'd dated cheerleaders like that. Angel wasn't really sure about the entire benefits and features thing. But he did understand that the general idea was that people are more interested in how something can change their lives than they are in whatever is behind that change.

The bell marked the end of the first week of school. As he watched the football team getting on the bus to go to the game, Angel realized how much of his life centered around football and the football team. Football wasn't just a game he played. For over half of his life, football had been who he was. He identified as a football player, outwardly to others – like in those ridiculous "get to know you" games that some teachers did at the beginning of a new school year – but also internally, to himself. He might say he was *on* the team, that is how people phrase these things, but the reality was more like he was attached to it. Being "*on*" something implied that you could step off at any time like you might step off of a skateboard or off of a bus.

Angel was attached to the football team. Attached, strapped in, and locked down. He was part of the team, and the team was part of him. The more stressful his life became, like during his parents' divorce, the stronger that attachment became. Angel wasn't just attached. He was clinging to it with everything he had. As he watched the last bag of footballs being thrown under the bus, he realized how attached he still was.

He missed the physical game, the running, the satisfaction of making a difficult catch, breaking a tackle. He was already missing the excitement of winning, and the team had not even played their first game of this season. But more than that, he missed the attachment to the team and to the game itself. His attachment was causing more pain than any injury ever had.

He watched the team bus and the object of his attachment pull away. Without football, who was he?

Angel really did not want to go home, but he had nowhere else to go. He had already decided that he was not going to say anything about seeing her at lunch. But his decision did not matter. She was not there when Angel got home at all. Angel checked the time on his phone. She was usually here by now. Good. This just made it easier to avoid the whole thing. Angel went upstairs to his room.

An hour passed. Then another. Angel still had heard nothing from downstairs. He looked around the house, more curious than concerned. She had gone out before, but she had always texted him to tell him she'd be home later. He fixed himself some ramen noodles and went back to his room.

Angel was glad to finally have this community service thing settled. He knew he still had to do the hours and the classes, but at least this part was finalized, and he could start to move through it. He was surprised by how much better he felt with just that small bit of resolution. He had not realized how much this whole thing was bothering him until it wasn't bothering him anymore. He played some Overwatch, but not as late as he used to. He ended up falling asleep around midnight. It was the earliest he had fallen asleep in some time, since way before this whole thing began.

He woke up to find that he had slept much later than he thought. It had been a long time since he had slept past noon. Angel rubbed his eyes and went downstairs.

She was not at the table. Not only was she not there drinking coffee like she should have been, but there was also no sign that she had even been home at all. No purse on the countertop; no shoes by the door. He checked his phone. There were no messages or missed calls. "She must have been home and then left again before I got up."

Or maybe not. Angel slowly opened the door to Delores's bedroom so he wouldn't wake her up. He saw the perfectly straight, perfectly unslept in bed. She was not home. She had not been home. He heard himself make a sound that he hadn't made in a long time.

"Mom?"

11

Not All Long Weekends Are Holidays

Angel wasn't sure how to feel about Mom not being there. It wasn't like they spent Saturday mornings together baking cookies. It was more like there was something out of place, like a missing sock. Not like lost car keys that you absolutely have to find. More like a familiar object that was not where it should be. He felt terrible for thinking it, but, honestly, he felt a greater sense of urgency about finding his phone when he left it in the band room than he did about the fact that his mother was missing.

"The band room," he thought. *"That graph thing was crazy..."* Angel wondered where "find your missing mother" fell on The Roberts Graph of Expectations and Hope. How had Roberts described the quadrants? At what point should he avoid open windows? In his head, Angel pictured a similar graph for Want and Need. He was pretty sure Mom would not be very high on the "Need" axis. He could take care of himself just fine. What he couldn't decide and did not want to think about was where Mom's coming back home would fall on the "Want" axis.

It didn't feel urgent, but it also did not feel right. Something was missing even if there really wasn't much to miss. It was a lot like the first time she went out on a date after Dad left. He didn't want to think about what she was doing on a date any more than he had wanted to think about what she might be doing now.

Angel put a burrito in the microwave and watched it slowly spin. He decided that if he really wanted to know where Mom was, he could just ask. He took out his phone and sent a quick text.

Where are you?

Then he went back to watching the slowly twirling burrito. He opened the microwave before the first ding ended. As he chewed the first bite, he walked to the bathroom and knocked on the door just in case she was in there. The unlatched door swung open on the first knock.

He contemplated the empty space where he had thought, for a moment, his mother might be. "Not there either," he said to the unoccupied toilet. "That's probably a good thing." He took another bite of his breakfast. "That could have been awkward."

He took the last bite of his burrito and wondered if the team won their first game. Last night's game was away. That meant that today's JV game would be at home. High school football teams alternate like that. The host of the Friday night Varsity game – the game that mattered – traveled to the visiting team's home field for the JV game the next day. Today's game would start at 1:00. Angel glanced at his phone. It was a little past 12:30 now. And, by the way, no new messages from Mom. He could still make it if he wanted to go to the game. That might be fun, in some weird, emotionally self-injurious kind of way. And Coach did not coach the JV team, thankfully. He probably wouldn't be there, but his friends from the team probably would be. With Coach not there, they might even speak to him.

Even better, JV games were free. And they were usually entertaining, even if they weren't exactly full of great feats of athleticism. These guys were still learning. At least they cared enough to try. Angel wasn't sure if he would have played football if he hadn't made Varsity as a freshman. He never played JV.

The stadium was not close to full, just a few parents and some random kids sitting in small groups spread around the bleachers, a holdover from when social distancing was a thing. There was no band in the stands for JV games. His former teammates were sitting in the bleachers in a non-socially distanced cluster near the 50-yard line, ready to cheer on their young apprentices. Angel walked on the first row of bleachers, putting one foot in front of the other on the same bleachers that he would have been running on at practices if he had stayed on the team. The aluminum bench seemed wide compared to the tightrope he had been walking the past few weeks.

He was about halfway there when he saw Coach sitting a few rows behind the team. Angel thought about just stopping and sitting on the bleacher where he was. He thought about leaving the stadium altogether. He briefly considered the idea of sitting right next to Coach but decided this was not the place for that conversation or the kind of confrontation that would probably ensue. Still, he missed his friends on the team. Marcus, another running back, was sitting on the edge of the team cluster, about four rows down from Coach. Angel could just sit there.

He sat down and leaned his head towards Marcus. "Hey."

Marcus nodded his head to acknowledge that he had heard. He did not look at Angel. He did not speak to Angel. A couple of the other football players turned and looked. Then they looked up into the bleachers at Coach. Then other heads began to look first at Angel and then at Coach. It wasn't long before the entire team looked like they were watching a slow-motion but rapidly accelerating tennis match. Coach said nothing. He just slowly shook his head. No one said anything. They didn't have to. Everything had already been clearly communicated to the team and to Angel.

Angel watched as the JV version of the Hoag High School Saints took the field. If this was a Varsity game, the band would have played *The Saints Go Marching In* as the team ran onto the field to cheering hometown fans. The JV team got the JV cheerleaders singing instead. None of them were in the choir. It showed. The Saints won the coin toss, elected to receive, and then promptly fumbled the ball beneath a pile of green jerseys near the 30-yard line. Nothing like starting the game with a turnover. The other team's offense took the field.

Angel leaned towards Marcus again. "That was interesting."

Marcus glanced back up at Coach and said nothing.

No one scored any points in the first quarter.

By half time, the Saints JV trailed 21 to 0. No band for JV games meant no half time show. The JV cheerleaders were doing what looked almost like a dance routine on the field with about the same degree of proficiency as the JV football players. Rah freakin' rah.

Angel looked straight ahead and spoke. "Well, this has been fun. I'm going to get something to drink. See you later."

Silence. Marcus stared at the field.

"Whatever, man." Angel shook his head, looked up at Coach, and walked away.

Angel was walking the balance beam first row of bleachers again when a feminine voice said, "Hey." He stopped when he heard that same voice again, only a little louder. Angel looked up the bleachers and saw the two kids who were posing with the dumbbells in weights class, the one that changed clothes in the music library instead of using the locker room and her... what? Boyfriend? *Why would she say hi to me if she was here with her boyfriend?" Doesn't that break some kind of girl code?*

The girl looked different today, much different than she had in the weights room. She was still just as skinny. She was young, about 14, Angel guessed, but he only guessed that because she was in high school. If he hadn't known she was in high school, he might have thought she was even younger than that. But her makeup and hair showed advanced cheerleader-level expertise. And the way she carried herself showed character. Pride, maybe? Confidence? Definitely some kind of attitude, but not in a bad way. Skyler wasn't exactly Angel's type – he usually went for the Blonde And Looks Great With Pom Poms girls – but she looked friendly enough. Her eyes and her smile had a kind of playfulness that was not included in the Saints Cheerleaders makeup palette. Hashim sat beside her, trying not to laugh but only marginally succeeding.

It was nice to see some friendly faces, even if Angel didn't know their names.

"Hi," Skyler said when she saw she had Angel's attention.

"Hey." Angel thought he could use the company. And he wasn't ready to go home and deal with all that. He sat down on the bleacher in front of Skyler.

75

"I'm Skyler. He's Hashim. We're in your weights class." Hashim giggled. Skyler, clearly the more mature of the two despite being younger, slapped Hashim's leg without even looking at her friend.

"I thought I saw you in there. You were curling dumbbells." Angel said. Skyler blushed. Hashim rolled his eyes and buried his face in his hands. Angel smiled at their reactions. "Aren't you both in the band?"

Hashim leaned forward to look around Skyler. "Yeah. She's the drummer. I play bass." Without looking at one another, the drummer and the bass player bumped fists.

Skyler smiled at Angel. "We're here just watching the guys."

"Yeah, me too."

"No. You're watching the game." Skyler laughed. "We're watching the *guys*." "Guys" was apparently a two-syllable word in Skyler-speak. Hashim shot a look and a grin at Skyler. What had been giggles exploded into outright laughter. It was his turn to slap Skyler's knee.

Angel allowed himself a small laugh. *"Okay ..."* – he thought. *"I guess she's not his girlfriend."* Angel suddenly wasn't sure how he felt about sitting by these two band geeks. The football team had names for people like Hashim, and most of those names would have nothing to do with Hashim being Black, although several of the Saints football players had names for that physical characteristic as well. *Why do girls hang out with gay guys? Is it so they don't have to do anything?*

He thought about saying goodbye and walking away. But social isolation is a powerful force, especially when you've been banished from your tribe. Angel missed having someone to talk to. He decided that he didn't want to spend the rest of the conversation looking back over his shoulder, so he moved up a bleacher and sat down by Skyler. The move was not enough to really get a conversation going. None of the three could really think of anything to say. But Angel didn't mind the quiet. It was comfortable, much more comfortable than the deafening silence he'd been getting from the team and the cheerleaders all week.

The three of them sat there for the rest of the game. Angel made occasional comments about what was happening on the field or how a play should have worked. He mansplained a cheerleader stunt. Hashim and Skyler whispered back and forth and pretended to be interested.

The home team scored some points, but it wasn't enough to win the game.

Angel was still sitting beside Skyler as the team filed out in front of them. Angel looked at his feet, then to the side, anywhere just so he would not have to look at the team as they passed. Skyler and Hashim had their heads down, too. They were whispering, but their eyes were on the guys. There were some glances from the team, a few double takes, some head shakes, but no comments. To speak would have meant breaking the team's apparent code of silence. No one said a word. Angel looked up just as Coach walked past. Coach looked right at him and shook his head.

"Okay," Skyler said. She leaned back and nodded towards the team. "I don't know what *that* was, but it was weird."

Angel shook his head. "It was nothing."

Hashim looked at Angel. "Looked like something to me."

Angel stood up and looked at the backs of his former teammates as they walked away. "I have to get home. Guess I'll see you Monday in weights." Skyler mistakenly assumed that the disappointed tone of his voice was directed at her.

Hashim elbowed Skyler and gave her a look that said, "*Say something!*" "Yeah, sure," Skyler said. "Whatever. See you then."

Skyler and Hashim watched as Angel walked away. Hashim spoke first. "Why do you have to be like that?"

"Like what?"

"Like *that!*"

Skyler watched Angel walk away. Then she looked at her friend, her bass player, her confidante. "Exactly where did you think that was going to go? Besides, it's not like you were stepping up either."

"He did not sit down here to talk to me. He sat next to *you*. He probably doesn't even know how to spell LGBTQ."

"You can't tell me there aren't gay guys on that football team."

"Oh, trust me," Skyler grinned. "There are gay boys on that team. They just don't know they're gay yet."

They both laughed.

Mom was sitting at the kitchen table when Angel got home. No drink. No phone. Just sitting, staring out the window. Angel walked past her and went to the fridge. She said nothing.

Angel closed the fridge and walked to the table. He started not to speak but could not resist the urge to ask.

"How was your night?"

"It was a night."

"Do anything?"

Mom looked up at him. Then she stood up and walked away. Angel listened as she quietly closed her bedroom door.

"Whatever." Angel went to his room and closed the door behind him. The housemates managed to avoid each other for the rest of the weekend.

12

Fridays Should be Fun

Weekends were the worst for Delores. In high school and college, both of which were more years ago than she cared to think about, Friday night was date night, or game night, or some kind of night that did not involve staying at home. As a young counselor, Friday night was when she could forget about her clients for a few hours without having to think about the problems that were scheduled for tomorrow. When she was married, Friday night was date night, especially once Angel was old enough to be left without a babysitter. Saturdays offered that same kind of freedom, but could not match the sense of relief that came on Friday. Friday was the joy of finding land after clinging to a raft in the ocean in a hurricane. It was the victory of crossing the finish line. Saturdays were the downtimes between races. Necessary, enjoyable, but not as thrilling as that first realization that she had survived another week. Sundays were spent bracing for the next storm.

Since the divorce, Fridays were just one more of those things that she wasn't able to enjoy as much as she had before. To be sure, these Fridays were better than the horrible Friday nights of the last few years of her marriage, when she sat home wondering where her husband was and who he might be with. Anything is better than that. But now, instead of date night, Friday was a reminder that she didn't have a date that night. It was more like the eye of the hurricane, and not a very big eye at that, instead of the end of the storm. Saturday nights were even worse. Only Sunday, with its feel of impending dread, remained the same.

When the gorgeous young man who was apparently an intern somewhere in the building asked her if she had plans for Friday night a few weeks ago, she decided almost immediately that she didn't. By the end of the week, that young intern *was* her plan. At 7:00 on that first Friday evening, that plan was in full effect.

Her Fridays and her plans for them changed significantly after that. Still, she always managed to get home in time to be ignored by Angel when he came down for breakfast.

Until today.

Waking up on a Saturday afternoon in a bed that wasn't her own had not been part of that plan. As the intern slept, she found his wallet and checked his driver's license. Somewhat embarrassing, but she was glad to know that she had not committed a felony. The absence of a credit card and very little cash underscored his status as an unpaid intern.

It was already after noon. She wondered if Angel had noticed she wasn't there. The thought that he might not even know was comforting and crushing at the same time.

The intern was still sleeping when she left.

13

Monday

She was sitting at the table when Angel came down for breakfast, watching the rain hit the window. She sipped her coffee and scrolled her phone while Angel walked by.

Neither acknowledged the other's presence.

She looked out the window as if she was looking for something out there somewhere. "It seems to be raining a lot lately."

Angel pretended to look for something in the fridge.

She looked into her coffee mug. "I am so tired of the rain."

Angel closed the fridge and picked at the magnets on the door. He hadn't noticed any dramatic changes in climate. It rains. That's what happens when summer is turning into fall. It rains.

He rearranged the magnets. "It was sunny on Saturday."

She smiled. It was a sad smile, just the same. "Yes, it was." She looked back out the window. "But then it started raining again."

"Are we going to talk about this?" Angel asked quietly and without looking away from the fridge.

"There's nothing to talk about." She took a sip of coffee to signal that was all she had to say.

"I guess not." Angel looked at the woman at the table. "OK. I'm going to school." He left without eating anything.

Leaving home early meant getting to school early, or at least early for Angel. The ostracizing social clusters were fully regrouped after being back in school for only one week. You'd never know they'd been on break. He saw Hashim and Skyler at the table with some other band geeks. He quickly nodded his head as he walked by but did not slow down to talk. He sped up his pace before he disappeared down the hall.

Skyler looked at Hashim. "See? What did you think was going to happen with that?"

Despite not wearing his earbuds, Angel still only managed to hear only about half of what anyone said during his first two classes. It was as if his personal volume control was on mute with only parts of the sound managing to occasionally break through the filters. He thought about his mother. He thought about the football team, which had somehow managed to reject him today even more than they had rejected him last week.

"They're probably mad about losing the game. They would have won if Coach would let me play."

Mostly he thought about nothing at all. His mind was as blank as the expression in his eyes. He was so overwhelmed with anger and other emotions he couldn't even name that everything inside had just shut down. He was making his way to third-hour English, not paying any attention to anything, when he almost ran over Clarissa as they both went through the door at the same time.

"Sorry." It was all he could think to say, but it was still more than he had said to anyone else so far that day.

"That's OK." Clarissa tried to remember if she had ever talked to Angel before they met in the band room last week. They were in the same grade. Surely they had been in at least some classes together before now. But she could not think of any other conversation they might have had. They both went into the room and took their seats. Angel tuned out this class just like the two he had tuned out before. The monologue inside his head was louder than anything in his environment.

Clarissa may not have known much about Angel, but she knew enough about people to tell that something was bothering him. Really bothering him. If he was a friend, she would have been worried. When class was over, she slowed her semi-sprint to lunch and waited in the hallway for Angel to unknowingly catch up to her. She couldn't think of anything to say, so she went with the first thing that came to mind.

"Are you going to the band room after school?"

Angel nodded his head but didn't say anything.

"I mean, I kind of overheard a little of what you were saying on the stage the other day. Sorry if I wasn't supposed to hear that."

"Doesn't matter," Angel sighed. "Yeah. I'll be there. I have to work in the file room or library or whatever he calls that room."

Clarissa didn't want to laugh, but she couldn't help smiling a little. "I personally call it the Chamber of Horrors, but I'm a little OCD, so it probably bothers me more than it should. But it really is a mess. Mr. Roberts would say that organization is not a high priority in his life. That's actually an understatement."

Angel showed his first faint smile of the day. "Yeah. I kind of noticed that."

"He's not highly structured, but he's a great teacher," Clarissa said. She was trying to find anything positive to say. She could tell that she was not doing a great job of lifting Angel's spirits.

"I guess." Angel also struggled for words to add to the conversation. "The band sounds good when you play at our games." That was the best he could do, and he even managed to get that wrong. "The games, I mean. Their games. I'm not playing this year."

"You quit football your senior year?" She immediately regretted even asking the question, especially since she already knew the answer. She could not imagine how it would feel to quit band during her last year of school or what could possibly happen that would make her do such a thing. She didn't know much about Angel, but she knew that he was all about sports. You could just look at him and tell that. The guy's face and body just screamed, *"I am an athlete,"* and that was not a bad thing. Not a bad thing at all. If only bodies like that weren't always attached to the same kind of brains.

"I couldn't make the practices." Angel shrugged. "That's just how it worked out."

Clarissa was glad to reach the end of the hall so she wouldn't have to make an excuse to leave. "I guess I'll see you in the band room."

"Yeah."

Angel spent his lunch sitting in his car. He did not want to eat lunch at school, did not want to go anywhere, and definitely did not want to go home on the off chance that she might be there for some reason. Who knows? She may have decided not to go to work at all today. Angel did not want to take that chance.

He spent fourth-hour biology thinking about how he was not looking forward to weights class. How is it possible for an hour to drag on forever and yet to be over before you know it? The bell rang. *"Here we go,"* he thought. He considered skipping weights but decided to go ahead and go. In his mind, the school was now linked to the court through his community service, even though there was no official connection between the two other than the agreement to do his ninety hours in the band room. He knew that on some level. But he could not shake the feeling that getting in trouble at school would only add to his legal problems. He should probably just stay out of trouble and get through this.

He paused in front of the weight room door, then he saw Coach.

"Angel!" Coach's voice boomed as Angel entered the weight room. It sounded ominous. "How was your weekend?" Coach taunted.

If you only knew, Angel thought, but all he said was "fine." He made his way to the squat rack and started putting weights on the bar. He heard Coach's voice from across the room. He was talking to Skyler, who was picking up the same 10-pound dumbbell she used all last week.

"You're going to have to lift more than that if you want to pass this class," Coach said. "Come over here to the bench press. Let's see what you can do."

Skyler had been dreading this day. All she wanted to do was to get through weights class without being noticed and without making her biceps any bigger than they already were. Her body and the mass quantities of testosterone it was suddenly producing were not cooperating. She avoided mirrors unless she was fully dressed.

"Coach, I really don't want big arms." She wasn't exactly pleading, but it was close, somewhere between asking for understanding and begging for mercy. Angel was trying not to listen, but the sound of Skyler's voice made it hard not to.

"Let's go, *son*."

The accented hissing syllable hung in the air before it smashed into its target like weights dropping to the floor from a deadlift.

"Did Coach just call Skyler 'son'?" Angel looked at the girl he sat next to at the game and tried to figure out what just happened. What did Coach just say? And why would he say that? Skyler was skinny and young, but she did not have a boy's face. Her voice did not sound like a boy. She did not act like a boy.

Skyler saw Angel's face and hated Coach even more for outing her, for making a decision that should have been hers and hers alone. She swallowed hard, held her head a little higher, and hoped that no one in the room had heard him but knew that everyone probably had. It was one of her recurring nightmares; middle school PE all over again. She may have been only 14, but she was not going to let this man make her cry. Or afraid.

She faced Coach head-on. "I am not your son."

Shit, Angel thought. Skyler might be a girl, but that took hella balls. Nobody talked like that to Coach. *Holy shit.*

Coach looked Skyler in the eyes. She returned his gaze, an equal but opposite reaction to his action. Skyler didn't say anything, but it was clear she was not backing down. Without breaking his stare, Coach pointed to the bench. "Get on that bench press and get to work."

Angel heard Hashim whisper, "Sky…".

What just happened here? Angel looked at Hashim, who seemed to be taking this even harder than Skyler. He was just standing there, like someone watching his best friend drown while wishing he knew how to swim. Angel thought about Skyler going into the band room to change. He thought about Skyler and Hashim at the game and how Hashim was obviously her best friend. About how they said they weren't dating. He had assumed it was because Hashim just wasn't into girls. That alone was hard enough for him to get his head around. He was sure he was right about Hashim. He was not sure about what he had assumed about Skyler.

Skyler took her anger out on the bench press, lifting with faster and faster reps until Angel thought she was going to get hurt. He could tell she was about to max out. She was an inexperienced lifter, and no one was spotting for her. Angel watched as the reps got gradually slower and more strained. The bar began to tilt to the left as Skyler's right arm pushed higher. Then the weights stopped rising at all. They began to sink while Skyler strained beneath the increasingly unstable barbell. Angel ran to the spotter's position, grabbed the bar, and put it safely on the rack.

"You didn't have to do that." Skyler's response to Angel reflected the anger she felt towards Coach.

"I know," Angel said as he walked to the side of the bench. "But it's my turn to get on the bench press."

Skyler sat up and pointed to the clock. "May I go change? *Sir?*" She released the last word with a vengeance, an echo of Coach's own inflection against her.

Coach looked at the weight room clock, then at Skyler, and then back to the clock.

"Just go."

Angel was not sure what he had just witnessed, but he knew he had not seen anything like this before. He looked back at Hashim, who was still in shock. Angel took Hashim's dumbbell from the floor and returned it to the rack. Angel looked at Coach and shook his head. Coach looked back at Angel with an angry stare.

"Next time, don't be a hero. Let the bar fall before you pick it up."

14

All The World Is A Stage

Skyler walked past Coach and out of the room with her head up and her shoulders back. There was no posturing or posing for the benefit of others, no exaggeration for dramatic effect. This wasn't a show. This was the pure power that came from a sense of confidence in who she was; pride in the best sense of the word. She maintained her dignity and her anger all the way to the band room.

Roberts could tell something had happened as soon as his drummer entered the band room.

"May I go to the stage, please?" Skyler asked quietly.

Roberts had no idea what had happened, but Skyler's seething expression told him everything he needed to know at that moment. He unlocked the stage door and held it open for her.

"Let me know if you need anything, OK?"

"Thank you. Right now, I just need to be alone."

Roberts went back to the band room. Students were already getting out their instruments. Hashim came in. His face amplified what Skyler had not said.

"Did Skyler come in here?"

"She's on the stage. Leave her alone." Roberts assumed Hashim was involved in whatever had happened to Skyler. Hashim did not wait for an answer from Roberts. He walked towards the door to the stage.

"No!" Roberts stepped between Hashim and the door. Hashim took another step. Roberts was more emphatic, if not as loud.

"I said, 'No.'"

The natural scowl and intense eye contact that Roberts had spent a career learning to soften were now on full unguarded display. Hashim had never seen Roberts when he was angry, but everyone had heard the stories. Hashim knew that he was dangerously close to experiencing this semester's eruption.

Roberts did not know what was going on, but he knew enough to know that he wanted to give Skyler some privacy. His voice was low and measured. "Don't go out there. Give her some space. You need to walk away." Roberts was very protective of his students. And right now, he was protecting Skyler from Hashim and anyone else who might hurt her.

Hashim realized what Roberts was thinking. "This wasn't some fight between us," Hashim argued.

Roberts was not moved. His eyes only became more intense. He stepped towards Hashim and spoke very slowly. "This is the part where you walk away." Hashim shook his head and walked towards his seat.

Roberts took a few seconds to regroup and to tone down what he knew had to be an intense expression on his face. Once he felt that his face was no longer in attack mode, he approached the still visibly angry Skyler.

"Skyler?"

There was no answer. Roberts took another step. "You OK? What's going on?"

"I'm fine." Skyler did not sound *fine.* "I just need to sit here a minute."

"Hashim wants to talk to you. Should I let him come out here, or should I just tell him that the jazz band needs their bass player right now?" Roberts slowly walked towards her. "And we could really use our drummer, too. I mean, I could play drums, but you know I'm not as good as you."

Skyler tried to smile. "That's true." She inhaled deeply, held it, and then exhaled. "I just need to sit here. Can I have a minute?"

"Do you want to go to the counselor?" Roberts was not really a fan of Ms. Carpenter, but he tried not to put his personal feelings for the school counselor on display for his students. There were probably some kids, somewhere, that she had helped, even if none came to mind. Certainly not any band or choir kids.

"God no," Skyler thought. Skyler just shook her head. She'd met with Ms. Carpenter before, and the woman insisted on deadnaming her. The so-called counselor was the next to the last person Skyler wanted to see right now, the absolute last person being Coach.

Roberts nodded his head towards the band room and spoke softly. "I have to get back in there." Then, in complete contradiction to what he had just said, he pulled up a chair, spun it around backward, and straddled it to face her. "Let me know if you need anything, OK?" Roberts stood up, looked at Skyler, and then turned to walk away. He looked back when he was at the door.

"You OK?"

Skyler did some quick nods with her head. "I'll be there in a minute. I just need to get myself together."

"Sure."

Roberts paused before he opened the door to the band room. One of the hardest parts of his job was pretending things were OK when things really weren't OK at all. He took a deep breath and opened the door. Most of the jazz band was already playing, just warming up. It sounded like a jazz version of after school practice, with blues scales instead of chromatic exercises. The noticeable exception, other than no one sitting behind the drums, was Hashim, who was sitting with his bass resting across his lap and his head down.

Clarissa was at the piano, playing through some lo-fi chord progression. Roberts walked over to the piano. "Wow," Roberts said. "That is really, incredibly, cheesy."

Clarissa kept her eyes on the keys. "I am all about the Major 7's." She smiled.

Roberts looked at the group. "Just keep on playing whatever you're playing," he told them. Clarissa looked up at him from the piano bench.

"You too. Keep playing," Roberts told Clarissa. She glanced up from the piano bench but started playing random arpeggios. Roberts spoke softly, careful to keep his voice beneath the other sounds in the room. "Has Hashim said anything?"

Clarissa shook her head as she played. "No. What's going on? Where's Skyler?"

"On the stage." Roberts paused. "I have no idea what's going on."

"Sorry. I got nothing."

Roberts walked over to the drums, picked up Skyler's sticks, and sat down. "Sorry about that. We need to play." What he meant was that *he* needed to play.

Jerry, a ninth-grade trumpet player, spoke up. "You're playing drums?" The rest of the band looked towards the drum set. "Where's Skyler?"

"She's not here." Roberts took a deep breath, regained a little more of his usual composure, and spoke to an obviously upset Hashim. "Give her a few minutes, and then you can check on her."

Roberts gave a four count. Nobody came in. "What?" he said. "You don't think I can do this?" Roberts was a drummer only in the most basic, "Yes, I can keep a beat" sense, a fact that he quickly admitted any time he had to play drums. He wasn't kidding when he told Skyler that he couldn't play as well as her. He did an intentionally loud and incredibly bad drum fill, which ended in a flourish with both sticks flying out of his hands. The older band members laughed. The younger players looked horrified. "Just kidding," he said as he collected the sticks from the floor. "I got this. Seriously. Let's play."

Angel spent his sixth-hour marketing class, trying to figure out what happened in weights. An hour ago, Skyler was just another girl. The most interesting thing about her was that she played drums and had a friendlier laugh than the cheerleader set. *I guess that wasn't the only difference.* He decided to deal with that later. First, he had to figure out Coach.

Coach had always been demanding. Some said he was mean. Angel believed it was because he wanted his athletes to be the best they could be. He was always telling people to work harder and to do more. There was nothing new about that. And he was always calling people "son," at least the guys on the team anyway. It was just a word Coach used. Angel had never really watched Coach around female students, but he assumed he would not have used a word like "son" if he was talking to a girl. Before all this started, Angel kind of liked it when Coach called him "son." But it was clear that Coach did not say "son" to make Skyler feel better. Just the opposite. The word was brandished as a weapon. And Angel could tell that it hurt Skyler to hear it.

Was it just an accident? Angel could see how, if someone knew Skyler as a boy, they might use the wrong pronoun. "Skyler" was one of those names that really could be for a boy or a girl. But it didn't sound like that when Coach was talking. It sounded intentional. It sounded like Coach meant for it to hurt. And Angel was pretty sure that Coach also meant for it to be heard by other people in the room. Especially him.

Was Coach just being a bully? Hoag High School had a big anti-bullying program. Coach had talked with the team about how athletes had to be extra careful because there was this unfair idea that his athletes were somehow bullying other kids, especially band and choir geeks. But wasn't this bullying? Bullying, as Angel understood it, was about picking on someone who couldn't defend themselves. It's about an imbalance of power. Wasn't that exactly what just happened?

But, wow. The way Skyler had stood up for herself was amazing. Nobody on the football team would have talked to Coach like that.

The idea that Coach did that to Skyler to somehow get to him just made Angel feel even worse.

Angel didn't know Skyler very well, but she seemed like a good person. She and that other kid at least talked to him when the team just walked away.

Right now, he was more interested in what Coach had said and how he had treated this kid. It wasn't right. It especially wasn't right if Coach was using Skyler to get to him. That was just wrong. He also wondered if it was going to happen again. And if it did happen, what was he going to do about it? True, he had grabbed the weights on the bench press before it landed in the middle of Skyler's chest. It was a good thing he was strong enough to make that lift. But he wondered if he would have the strength to do anything if Coach kept doing what he did today.

15

Pings

Three pings over the speakers meant there was about to be an announcement.

"Shh... Mr. Garcia's about to say something." Jerry was way too earnest for everyone's taste. He seemed to think it was his appointed duty to alert everyone to such things. Jerry stopped talking when he saw how the other jazz band members looked at him. It was another unspoken lesson in band room culture. Unfortunately, Jerry had already had several such lessons. Jerry wasn't a fast learner. Don't be a Jerry.

"Carpenter," Hashim said flatly while looking down the neck of his bass. He was still thinking about Skyler and the weight room. Hashim was beginning to look at his bass the same way Roberts looked at Fred. Clarissa thought it must be a guitar player thing. She didn't realize that she smiled at her clarinet the same way.

Ms. Carpenter's voice was next. "Students,"

"Told you." Hashim flipped the bass over and inspected the fretboard. "Mr. Garcia always does this disgusting hacking thing before

97

he speaks." The older students nodded their heads to confirm what Hashim said.

"Always."

"It really is disgusting."

"Like a cat with a hairball."

"I gag every time I hear it."

Roberts held up his hand. "Guys. I want to hear this."

The counselor continued, unaware of the conversations taking place over her disembodied voice. "Just a reminder that today is the last day to request changes to your class schedule. Any requests for changes must be made by the end of the day."

"Anyone dropping jazz band?" He slowly turned towards Clarissa, who had to be talked into playing the piano. It was not her favorite instrument. Clarissa sheepishly raised her hand.

Roberts knew she was joking. He hoped she was joking. "You are dead to me," he said in a voice with no expression. He was relieved when Clarissa laughed.

Hashim looked at the clock above the door. "Nice of them to tell us with thirty minutes left."

The pings motivated Skyler to leave the stage and go to the band room. Roberts saw her come through the door and met her halfway.

"You good?"

"Yeah." Skyler took the drumsticks from Roberts' hand. "Thanks." Roberts was glad to see the bass player and the drummer do their little fist bump as Skyler returned to her throne. The year when Hashim had gone on to high school and Skyler was still at the middle school had been hard for Skyler. They were the power rhythm section of the middle school jazz band. Not to mention mutually supportive friends. She spent 8th grade looking forward to being reunited with her bass player friend again.

In marketing class, the pings made Angel think about getting out of weights. He'd considered it before but had decided to stay. There was nothing else he could take that hour. Journalism required interviewing people, which meant talking to people, which did not sound like a lot of fun right now, especially since the football team and the cheerleaders weren't speaking to him. Stats would be way too much work. At least he understood weight lifting, even if it was getting harder to understand what was going on with Coach. He wondered if Coach's attitude was new or if the man had just always been this way, and he had never noticed before.

Skyler thought about her options for fifth hour. She had thought about dropping Coach's class last week but kept forgetting to go by the counselor's office, probably because it was nice to be in another class with Hashim. And if she didn't take weights, she would have to take PE, which wasn't any better. Even worse, changing her fifth hour would mean she would also have to drop jazz band, and that wasn't going to happen. Class schedules are like Rubik cubes. You can't just move one block without the other blocks getting pushed out of place.

Skyler had a new reason to stay now. How ironic. She had thought about dropping, but after today, there was no way she was going to let Coach push her out of that class, even if it was a class she did not like and did not want to take. For Skyler, this was no longer about lifting weights. It was altogether different now.

Roberts returned to his regular place in front of the band. "Skyler, the band does not seem to appreciate my abilities as a drummer. Your job is safe and secure." Everyone in the room enthusiastically agreed. Roberts looked at Hashim. "What's with the eye roll? I'm not *that* bad."

The jazz band read through a couple of more songs before it was time to go. Roberts quietly walked over to Skyler.

"What happened?"

"Coach." She nodded her head in the direction of the weight room. "I'll get over it. Or he'll get over it."

The bell rang. It was the end of the day. Roberts wondered how long it would take his newly conscripted librarian to show up.

16

Soloists and Rhythm Players

Angel was surprised by the lack of sound as he walked down the hall to the band room after school. He could usually hear them practicing as far away as the front office. He certainly should have been hearing it by the time he reached the band room doors. On this day, there was nothing. Angel walked into the band room and was surprised to see people just kind of hanging out. He knew that some of them were there from jazz band, but still. That kind of hanging around just did not happen in the weight room. You came in, you lifted, you left. Same with the gym. Was band just a social club? He did not know that for some students, the band room was the safest place to be.

It was Skyler who noticed him first. She managed an embarrassed smile.

"Thanks."

Angel did a quick nod. "No problem. Like I said, it was my turn on the bench press."

Roberts emerged from the library.

"Let's do this!"

The band geeks didn't laugh, at least not out loud, but they were clearly entertained by the thought of anyone venturing into the music library, especially someone who did not know what was waiting behind the door.

Angel followed Roberts into the smaller room. It was even more overwhelming than his first visit, probably because this time, he knew there would be no escape. "OK," Roberts pointed to a group of file cabinets. "Concert band music goes in here. Those are the big sheets." He pointed to another group of file cabinets. "This music, these small sheets like this, are for football and basketball games. Pep band music, marching band music, stuff like that. The jazz band stuff goes there. You can tell jazz band by the font. Over here," he pointed to the file cabinets on the other side of the small room, "this is where we put the choir music. You can tell it's for choir because it has words."

"Well, duh."

"There are different types of choirs, but don't worry about that now. That will sort itself out as we go."

Angel looked at the stacks, piles, and spills of paper. "This is a lot of paper."

"Yes. This represents the death of many, many trees." Roberts felt embarrassed and kind of guilty about asking Angel to do what really was his job. Then again, he was helping Angel get through this community service thing. At least that was how he had decided to rationalize it. It was a mutually beneficial relationship.

"This is many years of music that should have been filed a long time ago. I take music up like I'm supposed to, most of the time, after a concert or a season, but I usually forget to put it away. And some pieces just get tossed in here in random piles."

Angel looked around. "Random is a good word for this."

Roberts took a deep breath. "And I always think that this year will be different, that I will file it away and make this room look like a grownup works here. But that doesn't seem to happen. I don't know why." Roberts wasn't a hoarder, exactly, even if the room looked like a documentary about people with compulsive hoarding disorder. He actually threw away a *lot* of illegal copies of music and other pieces of paper every year. The kids knew they were illegal because they had COPYING IS ILLEGAL printed across the pages he had copied. He turned an apologetic face towards Angel. "I just don't put things away at the end of the year like I should. It's ... complicated. And then it became overwhelming." He took a deep breath. "At some point, I just gave up."

"Anyway..." Roberts opened his arms and turned back and forth as if presenting the room before an audience. He was P.T. Barnum in an extremely cluttered center ring. "Here it is. Let's get started."

"And, sorry, but by 'Let's,' I meant 'you.'"

In the central part of the band room, students were starting to practice on their own. A trumpet here, then a clarinet, then more, the same way that a hard rain begins with just a few random drops, except this didn't crescendo into pleasant white noise like rain. It just got louder. Like the paper in the file room, the sounds just piled up.

Angel's heart sank.

———————————

The rest of the week was remarkable only in that it was so incredibly unremarkable, especially given how the week began. With the deadline for schedule changes past, Roberts temporarily suspended his performance art "Music was your first language" show. No more accosting random students in the hallway. That performance would be reprised in December when students were deciding what to do next semester. There was no drama in the weight room, not because Coach or Skyler were respecting one another's boundaries but because both of them were waiting for the other to cross a line. Coach was back to not speaking to Angel, which was just fine with Angel. Hashim had been in and out of love at least twice without ever declaring the objects of his affection, which was fairly typical for Hashim by the second week of a school year. Even Angel had settled into a regular routine of working in the music library after school, depressing and soul-crushing though that routine might be.

There was a little excitement when Rachel, a tenor sax player, did a decent job on an improvised solo, after which she declared her love for her tenor sax and its superiority over all other instruments.

"Honestly, I do not understand why anyone would want to play a non-melody instrument like bass."

Silence fell over the band room. Everyone looked at Hashim except Skyler. She just looked at Rachel. "You do realize that Mr. Roberts is a bass player, right? Like, that he put himself through college playing bass?"

Clarissa piled on. "And he plays with some classic rock band with a bunch of old guys." She turned to Roberts. "No offense."

"None taken, but we're not limited to classic rock. *That* part was offensive." Roberts did an exaggerated eye roll so she would know he was kidding. Then he looked at Hashim. "Do you want to take this?"

Hashim looked at his bass with even more affection than usual. Then he looked at Rachel. "You may feel the groove, Karen. I *am* the groove. It's like being the catcher on a baseball team. If he's doing his job, nobody even knows he's there. But if he screws up, everybody notices. They might even lose the game." He looked even more intensely at the tenor player. "Or, in your case, if I intentionally change up the bass line on your next little showboat solo, I'll still look amazing, and people will think that you and your tenor sax really suck." Skyler reached across the top of her drums to fist bump Hashim.

Roberts smiled. He decided to let Hashim slide on the "Karen" comment this time. He usually did not take sides in these conversations, but this was *bass* they were talking about. "That's not exactly how I would have said that, but he's right. You do not want to upset the bass player. That's why we throw him cookies when rehearsals run long. Occasionally a pizza." Roberts was back in street preacher mode, only more preachy than when he was telling kids in the hall that music was their first language. "There is no relationship in music, nay, even in all of humanity, quite like the relationship between a drummer and her bass player."

"True that," Skyler agreed.

Roberts walked over to Rachel and smiled. "But, to be fair, that *was* an excellent solo. Remember when you hated improvising? You worked on it, and you got better. You deserve to be happy, even if you're not a bass player." Rachel laughed at the idea that she would be happier if she played bass.

Roberts looked at the clock. "OK. Good rehearsal. Put your stuff away."

As if to prove the fundamental importance of the rhythm section, Hashim and Skyler launched into a strong bass and drum groove. They were still playing when Angel walked into the room to work in the library. The former football player stopped to listen.

"They're good." He kept listening. "Like, *real* good."

"Yes, they are." Roberts imagined what he could do with this duo behind the jazz band. Hashim had told him last year about this incredible drummer that was coming up from middle school.

Hashim was telling the truth.

17

Into The Cave

Roberts was still admiring his new rhythm section when he realized Angel was not there to listen to the music. "How's the library coming along?"

"It's still a mess."

"I'm sure you're doing the best you can." He looked in the library. Angel had made some progress, but the room would still qualify for disaster relief. "There's kind of a learning curve. You'll get better the more you do it. Or if the circumstances change, like if I stopped talking, so you could work."

"That might help." Angel was smiling but not smiling.

Roberts said nothing for a few minutes. Then he thought he would try again. "Everything comes down to experience, circumstances, and attitude. It all comes down to these three things."

After a short pause, he added. "And you've had a good attitude about working in here, so that's good."

"Thanks." Angel had not heard the phrase, "You have a good attitude" for a while. He smiled when he realized that the compliment did make him feel slightly less annoyed by whatever it was Roberts was talking about. *I see what you did there, Roberts. Well played. But don't push it.*

They kept sorting and stacking pages. Roberts looked up. "Hear that?"

Angel listened. "I don't hear anything."

"Yeah. That's what I mean. A band room is not supposed to be that quiet."

They stepped out into the empty room and its uncharacteristic silence.

Angel had an idea. "If they're gone, then we could set up a table out here and move some of this."

"Good idea. That would change our circumstances."

Angel pretended he didn't hear the comment about circumstances. He just wanted to get this done without having to listen to a lecture. He wanted to ask if this was going to be on a test, but he was afraid Roberts would launch into some rant about how life is actually the ultimate test.

They cleared guitar strings, valve oil, and other random items from the table, consolidating what had been on two tables of random parts and pieces of things into one. "You've heard these guys practicing. Are they doing the best they can do?"

"Some are better than others," he said, as he removed the last box of reeds from the table. "So, I would say no. At least not all of them."

108

"Grab that end." Roberts lifted his end of the table. "I *know* they are doing the best they can. That doesn't mean they can't get better. It's my job to make them better." He kept talking while they moved the table closer to the library. "But it's the best they can do with the experience, circumstances, and attitudes they have at that moment. That's where they are as musicians *and* as people."

No real response. Roberts put his end of the table down and decided to go in a different direction. "You're a really good running back, right?"

"I was." Angel shrugged. "Not anymore."

"What kind of experiences did you have that made you good at football?"

"A lot." Angel remembered his dad throwing the football to him before he was even in kindergarten. It was a bittersweet memory for many reasons.

"Exactly. Skyler and Hashim didn't get as good as they are without that same kind of work ethic. Experience is a long term thing. It's the accumulation of everything you've ever done, everything you've been through, and everything you've seen, the good and the bad. All of that goes into what you are doing, feeling, and even thinking right now."

Roberts went into the library and emerged with more music. "But even with all your experience, was there ever a night when it just didn't work? Ever a time when you just messed up?

"All the time."

Roberts looked at Angel. "Why?"

"I don't know. The weather, the other team played better, whatever." Angel stopped and remembered something Coach always drilled into his players. "But, you can't use circumstances as an excuse."

"You mean you can't blame circumstances when you didn't do the work or if you have a bad attitude."

Angel repeated himself as if Roberts just didn't get it. "Like Coach said, you can't use circumstances as an excuse."

"Because they're not an excuse." Roberts walked into the library to get more music to sort through. "Circumstances are as much a part of this as experience and attitude." He came out of the library and looked across the room at the racks of guitars by the opposite wall. "Think about a guitar player who practices all week. He knows the song, and he's ready to play. But when it's time for him to play the song for the test, he can't do it. Maybe he broke a finger. Maybe he didn't get enough sleep the night before. Maybe he's upset."

Angel looked at him. "Are you speaking from personal experience?"

"On all three counts." Roberts smiled and gently massaged the index finger of his left hand. "But the point is that even with all that practice, his ability to play guitar is changed by those circumstances."

Roberts circled the table with sheets of music that we're looking for a place to land. "Some circumstances don't change very quickly, like if you're sick or you don't have any money. Some may not change at all, like having some kind of disability or having a bad family situation."

Angel spoke softly. "Or wondering whether your mom will come home at night..."

"Exactly. Circumstances like that could definitely affect how you do something." What Angel said created a blip on Roberts' radar, but he was so wrapped up in explaining his ideas that he completely missed the not so subtle subtext about someone's mom not coming home. "It's one of those 'It's not your fault, but it is your problem' kind of things, like when someone crashes into your car, and you have to deal with that. Not your fault, but it is your problem.

Angel thought about how his senior year was going so far, and the bad circumstances that had changed his life so quickly and so much. Some of them were absolutely his fault. And others were exactly like Roberts said. Not his fault, but they were his problem. He wasn't sure which category covered his community service.

Roberts continued. "On top of all of that, on top of experience and circumstances, is someone's attitude at that moment. We act like all of this is permanent, that circumstances and attitudes are somehow hardwired. It isn't like that at all. Circumstances, attitudes, even the way we interpret our experiences, all of that constantly changes, from one second to the next. None of this is permanent."

"Life is impermanent."

18

Everybody's Just Doing the Best They Can

R oberts started writing on the whiteboard.

Angel rolled his eyes. "Another graph?"

"Even better. An equation!"

EXPERIENCE + CIRCUMSTANCES + ATTITUDE = OUTCOME

"Whatever happens, whatever someone does, everything comes down to their experiences, their circumstances, and their attitude. It all comes down to these three things." Roberts stepped back and admired his work. Then he turned to face Angel. "The way Coach treated Skyler in weights the other day and the way he reacted when you helped Skyler were the result of his experiences, his circumstances, and his attitude at that very moment. If any of these three things had been different, something else would have happened. Maybe better. Maybe worse."

"You heard about that thing in weights?"

"I hear everything, but that's not the point." Looking at the board, Roberts was quite pleased with his neat mathematical summation.

"Everyone is just doing the best they can, based on their experiences, their circumstances, and their attitude at that moment." He turned to face Angel. "Or at least most people are."

Angel was skeptical. "You're saying that Coach had no choice *but* to act that way. I can't believe that."

"It's not that he didn't have any choice. We can always choose to do the right thing or to do something else. It's more a question of what someone is most likely to do. I mean, a dog can walk on two legs, but he's not very likely to do that, at least not for very long. Eventually, he'll walk like a dog because, well, he's a dog."

Angel had seen Coach at his best, like when Coach pushed him hard or when he pushed a team to an unimaginable comeback win in the fourth quarter. "What Coach did to Skyler was not his best." Angel thought about it some more. "And it was intentionally not his best. He chose *not* to do his best."

"Or maybe Coach was doing the best he could, based on his experiences, the circumstances, and his attitude at the time." Roberts saw the anger in Angel's face. Before Angel could respond, Roberts continued his thought. "That doesn't make it any better," he said before Angel could say anything. "It was the wrong kind of best, like the best tornado to completely destroy somebody's hometown or the best fire to burn down a village." He looked at Angel. "A snake is doing the best he can when he bites you, but you're still going to die."

"He's been looking pretty angry since school started." A sad expression came over Angel's face. "It may be because of me."

"Stop." It was the same tone of voice Roberts used when he told Hashim to stay off the stage. "In no way is what Coach said to Skyler about you. Are we clear on that?"

"Yes."

"Good. This is not on you. This is on Coach and what he chooses to do with his anger or whatever his problem is."

Roberts sat back. "And even if he was angry, it doesn't take much to change what happened. Think about what a difference even a small thing, like changing someone's attitude, can make."

Roberts looked over at the guitars again. "I might ask a guitar player to take a test at 10:00. And he might not do very well at all."

Angel stopped him. "Is this the same guitar player who had the broken finger and wasn't getting enough sleep?"

"No. Different guy. Guitar players tend to have a lot of issues. Anyway, I can change his attitude by telling him he can do better or something. Then, when he tries a few minutes later, he's able to play it."

Angel still didn't think it was all about attitude. "Or you could change the circumstances by asking other people not to play while he's taking the test. That might make it easier for him."

"True. So when Coach did what he did at, let's say at 2:36 on a Monday or whatever time it was, that was the best he could do with the experience, circumstances, and attitude he had at that exact instant. But what if something happened that changed his attitude? Or the circumstances, like you said? He might have done something completely different just a few minutes later. But whatever he did, that new thing would be the best he could do at *that* time, like at 2:40 or whenever that was. Who knows what might happen at 2:45?"

He looked at Angel. "Attitudes and circumstances can change just that fast. You are not the same person you were when we started this conversation. Neither am I. People are constantly changing. Nothing is permanent."

Angel looked almost angry. "I'm surprised you would give him a pass like that."

Roberts shook his head. "I'm not giving him a pass at all. Just because it was the best he could do at that moment does not make it any less wrong." He paused. "But I have to believe that *most* people are trying to do the best they can *most* of the time. If I didn't believe that, I couldn't be a teacher."

Angel didn't think Coach was doing anything close to the best he could do. He wasn't interested in looking for ways to give the guy a break. At the same time, he *was* beginning to think that his mother may be doing the best she could do with her experiences, circumstances, and current attitude, even if it was killing her and hurting him. She wasn't doing it to hurt him or even because of him. Instead, she was acting that way because that was how she decided to cope with whatever was going on in her head. Her experiences, circumstances, and attitudes were pushing her to do whatever she was doing with her life.

Roberts looked at the clock. He was a little embarrassed that Angel's community service work time had turned into a pedantic philosophical lecture. "Sorry I went on so long. This stuff fascinates me. You should probably be getting home. At least we got some work done. I'll mark this down as an hour, OK?"

Angel wanted to say that the time didn't matter. He was probably going home to an empty house and another night of not knowing what was going on with his mother. Those were his circumstances at this moment.

But he didn't. All that came out was, "Sounds good to me. Thanks."

Roberts stayed behind as Angel walked up the hall. He thought about all the pain and problems he could have avoided if he had known that most people really were just doing all they could do. They weren't intentionally cruel, or difficult or any of the things that were so frustrating for him when he was a young teacher. Then he reminded himself that those pains and problems are part of his experience. He wondered how different his life would be, for better or worse, if he did not have those experiences that led him to where he is now.

19

Another Weekend

As he had expected, Angel walked into an empty house. This had become the new normal. Mom had been making it home by 11:00 or so on weeknights for the past few weeks, but this was Friday night. Angel wondered if she would come home at all or just have another unannounced sleepover somewhere like she did last week. He thought about going to the football game. The Varsity team was playing at home. He could sit with the band, maybe bang on a cowbell while they played *The Saints Go Marching In* as the team would run on to the field. He didn't think Skyler would mind him being in the percussion section. The band would also play that Saints song for every touchdown… if there were any touchdowns this time. He'd heard the receivers did not have good hands and had no speed. They were having to use the run a lot, but they apparently weren't that good at that either. He decided just to order a pizza and play Overwatch instead. Another thrilling night in the life of an American teenager.

She came in around 9:30, about the time the game would have been finishing up. Go Saints. Her entrance was given away by a loud, unintelligible voice, followed by "Shhh…," and then by the sound of two people laughing loudly enough for Angel to hear them in his room upstairs. That was it, a poltergeist with a loud laugh. If he hadn't heard them, Angel probably wouldn't have known she had been home at all.

For the first time since he was six, Angel wished he had a dog. At least a dog could have growled or humped the guy's leg or something.

He wondered if she had gone to the game and if she even knew he wasn't playing this year. He decided the answer to both questions was, "Probably not." There were some other stumbling noises, more laughter, the sound of someone tripping over something in the dark, and a loudly whispered, "OK, let's go." The door shut, a car started, and the night was quiet once again. The poltergeist has left the building.

Angel thought about going out, but where would he go? And why? He could just drive around and see what was going on, but he wasn't sure he really wanted to know. If he was going to be alone, he might as well be alone in his own house and not in the company of others. He finished what was left of the pizza, played some more Overwatch, and went to bed.

He was awakened by the sound of the door again and laughter that was much less guarded than before. The poltergeist again. His phone said 2:39AM. *"The bars must have closed,"* he thought. He heard her laugh, followed by the same "OK. Let's go," only this time from a male voice, presumably the same male voice he had heard laughing before. Who knows.

At least he's not spending the night here. That rite of relationship passage had not happened yet, at least not at home. But Angel knew it was only a matter of time until he was greeted some morning by some guy in boxer briefs slurping milk from a cereal bowl over the sink. Or drinking from his grape juice bottle.

2:57. Twelve minutes. That was it. And she didn't even try to see him.

Mom was MIA all day Saturday, Saturday night, and all day Sunday. Angel did not see her again until Monday morning when his curiosity overrode his fear of the potential emotional scarring that might result from meeting her mother's boyfriend while the boyfriend was lying in his mother's bed. Or worse. He opened her bedroom door to see if she was home. She was sleeping. Alone. Thank God.

"Hey." Nothing. No response.

A little louder. "Hey!"

She rolled over. "What? Why are you in my room?"

"I thought you might want to get ready for work."

"Work? I don't work on Sundays. Get out of here."

Angel choked back whatever was rising in his throat. He did not want to deal with this right now. "OK. See you later."

She was still in bed when Angel left for school.

20

Another Monday

Angel told himself that his mother was doing the best she could do with the experiences, circumstances, and attitudes that were going on in her life right now. *Just doing the best she can.* He repeated that mantra all the way to school. But exactly which of those variables had to change to bring on all of this? He was trying to understand, but losing an entire day and staying in bed when you should be going to work had to be an incredibly low bar for the "best" of anything. He thought about his own expectations and hopes. He could not imagine how his expectations for her could possibly be any lower than they were right now. Unfortunately, his hopes were just as low. He thought about his first conversation with Roberts and about the graph of hopes and expectations. This seemed low on both. *Was this the quadrant where people should avoid open windows?* At least he didn't have to worry about being disappointed.

His morning classes were even more drab than usual. Clarissa asked how he was when she saw him in English class third hour. Judging by the concern in her eyes, Angel knew he must not have looked like he felt very good. But it was nice to know she cared, even if he didn't want to talk about it yet.

He wished he had more classes with Clarissa. She spent the entire afternoon in the band room, from fourth hour concert band, then fifth hour choir, and then jazz band sixth hour. Apparently, there were a lot of band geeks who did that. It had never occurred to Angel that you could or would even want to spend half the day in the same room. No wonder Roberts allowed his students to talk to him like they did. Or that he would speak with them like he did. If you spend two or three hours a day in the same room for four years, you're either going to love that room or hate everything and everyone in it. He was sure there was some drama – there is always drama at a high school – but there didn't seem to be any hate in the band room. He wondered what Roberts would do if there ever was a fight in there. Probably just tell everybody to do the best they could.

Monday was Hashim's turn to struggle with the bench press. Unlike Skyler, who was actively trying not to develop any muscle mass, Hashim was suddenly very interested in becoming as buff as possible. Unfortunately for Hashim, or, maybe, fortunately for Hashim, he didn't seem to realize what a painfully slow process that is. Angel wondered if there was a graph for confidence and knowledge, where would Hashim's dot for building muscle mass be? Overconfident and uninformed?

Coach seemed very interested in whatever he was reading on his computer. Angel didn't know what it was, but Coach really did not seem to appreciate it very much. He kept slamming the computer closed, walking away, returning, and reading whatever it was again. Lather, rinse, and repeat. Coach was much less attentive in weights class that day, which was not a bad thing. Not bad at all, really, so long as nobody dropped some weights on their foot or something.

"Yes, Skyler. That machine is for developing pecs." Coach Angel to the rescue. *"Coach Angel,"* he thought. *"That has a nice ring to it."*

The bell rang. Only 78 more weightlifting days in the semester, but who's counting?

Clarissa stepped out of the band room when the bell rang and was standing by the door when Angel walked past. He saw her there.

"Hey." It was the best he could do.

"Hey." She looked at Angel's exhausted eyes. "You OK?"

"Yeah. It's nothing. Just looking forward to filing that music! Uggh."

"Been there, done that, no thanks," Clarissa said. "Freshman year. I was much more eager to please back then."

Angel smiled. "Really? Well, I wish I had known you back then." It was his first non-drab moment of the day.

Clarissa decided to ignore what he said. *I've been here for three years, and you pay attention to me now?*

"See ya'." She pivoted so hard he thought her hair was going to hit him. He watched as she went into the band room to get ready for jazz band. Today was going to be improv day, which meant that Clarissa The Reluctant Piano Player, Hashim, and Skyler would play the entire hour while the melody instruments took turns improvising over what they played. Hashim and Skyler loved it. Clarissa referred to it as "taking one for the team." Roberts loved improv, and he especially loved 12 bar blues changes. "Jazz is a conversation," he would say. "Let's converse!" Some soloists, like Rachel, were better musical conversationalists than others. Others, like Jerry, played the same two notes no matter what else was going on.

"Really, man?" Roberts said to Jerry. "I mean, seriously? Two notes? One prolonged trill? Rachel, please explain to Jerry how this is supposed to work." Roberts was real big on having students explain things to other members of the band. The younger students sometimes made the mistake of thinking it was because he was lazy. His older students knew he did it because the student who was explaining learned more about whatever it was when they had to explain it to someone else. They certainly learned more that way than they would have if they had to sit through him explaining the same things over and over again for four years, if they stayed in jazz band all four years. It was also Roberts' way of checking to see who really knew what they were doing and who was just faking it. He was teaching one group while testing another.

Clarissa filed all these little tricks away for future reference when she was out of college and was teaching a band of her own. She had learned a lot from Roberts about how to teach. She had learned even more about how not to teach high school students. For example, she vowed that she would *never* allow her band room to be this cluttered and unorganized. And she wasn't totally sure she could manage the kind of relaxed, unstructured environment that seemed to work so well for Roberts. She didn't believe that there were too many teachers anywhere who could manage that. Clarissa didn't know it, but there were days when Roberts wasn't sure he could manage it either.

The bell rang. Clarissa felt bad as she watched Angel walking through the door and into The Cave, the name he had given to the music library. He looked exhausted, way beyond being just physically tired. This was more than just not getting enough sleep. She was impressed when she heard how he had helped Skyler in weights. She thought that showed the best kind of strength. Yes, he was a jock, but maybe she had underestimated him. *And was he hitting on me in the hall before jazz band? Seriously? Are the cheerleaders just not an option anymore?*

Clarissa wasn't the only one to notice that Angel seemed to be going through something more than could be explained by having to spend an hour each day filing music. Although, that alone would be enough to make anyone feel depressed. Roberts noticed it. So had Skyler and Hashim. Even Rachel, not the most attentive observer when it came to other people's feelings, noticed that "that boy" who came into the room each day – "You know the one. The boy who did something and they almost put him in jail, but some bleeding heart judge let him go" – was looking kind of sad.

"What a Karen," Hashim said under his breath.

"True that," said Skyler.

Hashim pointed the top of his bass towards Rachel like an extended pointing finger. "Don't be a Karen."

Angel was not looking any better that afternoon. Clarissa was beginning to get worried. She didn't expect him to look rested. There is no nap time in high school unless you count history class. She just hoped he would look less worn down.

"I wish we could help him," she said to Skyler as everyone put away their instruments. At least with the piano, she didn't have to take the instrument apart every day like she did with her clarinet. The piano had that much going for it.

She decided to ask Roberts about it. "How did Angel end up having to file music?"

"You'll have to ask him. I don't know."

Clarissa looked skeptical. "Seriously?"

"He came and asked me if there was anything he could do in the band room. I was just glad to have someone who would work in there. That is all I know."

Clarissa pushed. "You have to know more than that."

"I'm not sure I really have to know anything more than that at all. But I do know that I do not talk to students about other students. And you should know that, too. I wouldn't talk to Angel about you."

"Ouch."

"Seriously," Roberts told her. "If you want to know, ask him. But try to do it on a day when he doesn't look like he just lost his puppy. He has not looked very happy lately."

Clarissa disagreed. "Those might be the days when he needs to be asked the most." She looked back at the library. "Does he have to work in there until it's finished, or is it more of a time thing?"

"These things tend to be based on hours and not on any particular type of work. I suppose if he finished up in there before he finished his ninety hours, he could do something else. But I don't see how that's going to happen." He looked as guilty as he felt about the condition of the library. "I mean, have you been in there recently?"

"I promised myself I would never go in there again after my freshman year."

"Exactly."

Ninety hours? Wow. Clarissa was surprised by the tremendous amount of time. She was more surprised that Roberts had let the number slip out.

Clarissa went to the stage to practice. Other students came in and put in their practice time. Roberts was working on the guitars, replacing broken strings, trying to adjust a couple of guitar necks. Angel was alone in his cave, where his experiences, conditions, and attitudes were making him move very slowly today. He felt exhausted even though he had been going to bed earlier than he could ever remember going to bed before. Just because you go to bed earlier does not mean that you're getting more sleep. And just because you're sleeping doesn't mean you aren't exhausted.

21

Not Your Fault But It Is Your Problem

Roberts looked at the clock and raised one hand to get everyone's attention. "It's 5:30. I have to get home and water my plants." From inside the library, Angel heard Roberts saying goodbye to the after school practice crowd. He did not want to leave, but he knew that he couldn't stay. Mom spent the last three nights at home, or at least Angel thought she had, but who knew when she would be there on any given night or even if she would be there at all. He'd stopped checking. They didn't even see each other in the kitchen anymore. He was getting used to living alone, but he didn't like it as much as he thought he would.

Angel came out of the library after everyone else left.

"I had forgotten you were in there." Roberts peeked inside the library door and looked around. "Looks like you've made some progress."

"Got a minute?"

Roberts looked at the clock. He had already been at school since 6:30 that morning with some students who couldn't stay after school. He hated to tell people they couldn't practice, especially if they were willing to come in an hour before school started. He didn't understand it, but some parents would not let their kids practice at home.

"Sure."

"I've been thinking about that whole *Doing the best they can'* thing. What do you do when someone's best just isn't good enough?"

Roberts felt the reaction in his face. "Is Coach being an idiot?"

"No. No, this has nothing to do with Coach. This is something else. This person isn't mean. I don't even think they're trying to hurt anyone. What you said made me think they are probably doing the best they can with their...."

They said the phrase together. "Experiences, circumstances, and attitudes."

Angel smiled. It was one of the few smiles he'd had that day. "Right. That."

"I'm impressed you remembered that conversation."

Angel continued, "They're just not doing their job. Like, literally. Not doing anything."

Roberts measured the possible distance between what Angel was saying and what he was trying to tell him. "It could be depression. They should probably talk to someone who can help them. Like, serious help. I'm a great listener, but I'm no counselor."

"Yeah. Neither is Ms. Carpenter."

Roberts tried not to laugh. "So, what's going on?"

Angel took a deep breath. "What do you do when someone's behavior is hurting them or could hurt them? And what if they could hurt you?"

Roberts' reflex was to ask the same question that he always asked when a student came to him with problems.

"Are you safe?"

Angel was surprised by the question. *Why would you think I wasn't safe?* "Yeah. This isn't about that." He wondered how Roberts defined "safe." Whatever the definition was, Angel did not feel unsafe. Just unsure.

Roberts ran through several possible scenarios in his head. *Is he talking about some friend of his?* Roberts wasn't sure what the situation was, so he decided to make his response equally vague. "Well… at some point, you have to decide whether the relationship is worth what it is costing you or what it would cost you to stick around. You can't fix them. Only they can do that. You can help, or offer to get them some help, but it's ultimately up to them."

Roberts sat down and motioned for Angel to do the same. "How much do you care about this person? How much are you willing to invest in this relationship? I mean, you have to decide if it's worth keeping them in your life and what it would cost to change the things you can change."

Angel noticed that Roberts seemed to be talking to himself more than he was talking to him. "We tend to stay in bad relationships, bad jobs…" Roberts glanced at Angel, then away… "bad situations…" His voice trailed off for a moment. Angel thought he saw Roberts move a little, like he was literally shaking something so he could finish what he was saying.

"We stay until the pain of staying is greater than the fear of leaving it behind." He paused, then smiled a little. "There's an equation for you." He laughed a little, one of those laughs that just say "huh."

Roberts looked straight ahead, his eyes fixed on some spot on the wall. "And sometimes that may mean deciding how much you hope to change, how much can even be changed." He paused. "How much do you want to *be* changed." He looked very serious, almost somber. "Because changing that person or that situation will absolutely change you."

He knew there was something Angel wasn't telling him. He just couldn't figure out what it was.

"And this isn't about Coach?"

Angel was so deep in thought about how sometimes you just have to let them go that he didn't respond right away. "No. It's not Coach. Something else."

"That's really all I have. Sorry. Sounds like another one of those, "Not your fault, but it is your problem" situations. Those happen a lot."

"Yeah. They do." These "*not your fault but it is your problem*" problems were turning out to be the hardest kinds of problems to solve. That whole, "*staying until the pain of staying was greater than the fear of leaving*" piece didn't really apply in his situation. He did not fear leaving his home or his mother. He had been looking forward to leaving just a few weeks ago, but leaving her and losing her were two very different things. If he stayed but did nothing, at what point would her problem become at least partially his fault?

22

With a Little Help From My Friends

Clarissa, Skyler, and Hashim waited for Angel in the parking lot. They weren't sure which car was his, but the possibilities became more evident as the lot cleared out. Eventually, there were only six cars left, and one of those belonged to Clarissa.

"Did we miss him? I thought he was right behind us."

"There he is." The Trio watched the solitary figure approach the cars.

"Were you working in that room all this time?" Clarissa couldn't believe that he'd stuck around for that long after they left.

"No. I was just talking to Roberts."

Hashim laughed. "Oh, I know those conversations. Did he turn his chair around and kind of rock back and forth?"

"Did it involve an equation?" Skyler hadn't been in high school long, but she already knew how Roberts was always putting things into equations. "I love the equations!" Her favorite "Roberts Equation" so far was "Intelligence is inversely proportional to the volume of the speaker."

It was amazing how often that equation seemed to hold up these days, especially with Coach yelling in weights class.

"Anyway…" Clarissa stretched the word as far as she could without breaking it. "We wanted to talk to you about something."

"OK," Angel was a bit apprehensive. In Angel's experience, that line rarely led to anything good.

The Trio looked at one another, deciding who should speak first. It turned out to be Clarissa. "We know you have to work ninety hours in the library." She paused, as though thinking of a side note. "Seriously, I took American Government last year. This seems like an Eighth Amendment violation to me. You should consider an appeal."

"I did and was told none would be forthcoming."

"Well, be that as it may, we talked about this and we," she pointed to the other two-thirds of the group, "want to help you out. I talked to Roberts. I mean, I didn't tell him what we were thinking of doing, but I did find out that your… what? Sentence? Is this considered a sentence?"

"Yes. I have been tried, convicted, and sentenced. Sort of. I mean, there was no trial. But this is what the judge told me to do. Case number 246-01. Was thinking of getting a tattoo of that."

Hashim and Clarissa laughed. "Seriously? That's your case number? You were prisoner 246-01?"

"Ooooh…" Skyler raised her hand and started hopping up and down. "Can I be Eponine? Let me be Eponine!"

Angel was not amused. Must be a band geek thing.

Clarissa stopped laughing. "Sorry. OK. Never mind. So, we talked to Roberts and he said that your sentence is about the number of hours you work, not what you do with them. He said he's done these things before and it doesn't matter what you do, as long as it takes you ninety hours to do it. So, even if you finished the library before the time is up..."

Hashim interrupted. "Which does not really seem humanly possible..." Clarissa and Skyler shook their heads to confer.

"Anyway, even if you finish filing all that music, you would still have to work off the rest of the ninety hours. That doesn't really seem fair to me, but that's what it is."

"Hence the whole Eighth Amendment thing..." Hashim added. Clarissa wasn't the only one who had read the Constitution.

"So, what are you saying? That I should work even slower because it doesn't matter?"

"No." Clarissa again looked at Hashim and Skyler. "We want to help you." Clarissa could not believe she was actually hearing her voice say those words. She hadn't stepped foot in the library in three years. The thought of it made her shudder all over again.

"That's nice, really, but I don't think Roberts would go for that."

"Roberts won't know until it's over. By then, it will be done. What's he going to do? Mess it up again so you have to fix it all by yourself? He'll just be thrilled to see the tops of those file cabinets again. It bothers him a lot more than he says it does."

Angel did not know what to say. This is the kind of thing that friends do. It is not the kind of thing that someone you met only a few weeks ago would offer. He wondered what it was going to cost him, but he didn't really want to ask.

Skyler sensed his hesitation and spoke up. "This isn't just for you. It's really for all of us. I haven't been here that long, and I can already tell it's a problem. He always has to look for stuff in there and he can never find anything. Besides, I kind of owe you one."

"You don't owe me anything."

Clarissa was clearly the leader of the group. "Here's what we talked about doing. Tell me if this works for you. Tomorrow night is an away game. The band isn't going, so we'll be in town. We'll just hang around after school and go in there after Roberts goes home. Will that work for you?"

Angel appreciated the offer, but he was skeptical of the plan. "How are you going to get into the band room if he's not there?"

"There's always something going on at the school at night. Town volleyball games, weight lifting, something."

She was right about that. People were in and out of the building all the time at night and on weekends. "Right. Getting into the building won't be a problem. But how will you get into the band room? He always locks that door."

"The janitor cleans at night. We'll go in when he's not looking. Or I'll tell him I need to get my clarinet. Something. We haven't worked out all the details yet. The main thing is, can you get away to spend the night in there?"

"You're going to spend the entire night in that room?"

"Well, I don't think we'll get it done in time to catch the 9:27 show at the movies. Yes. I think it will take all night. We can make it. Can you?"

"Trust me, I won't have any problem with not going home."

"Hashim? Can you make it?"

"Mom goes to work at eleven and doesn't get home until around 7:30." He turned to Skyler, then to Clarissa. "She's always there to fix my breakfast. So, as long as I'm home by 7:00, I'm good. And, honestly, I can just tell her I have to be somewhere in the morning just in case I don't make it home by 7:00. I could probably stay all day Saturday if I need to. I don't usually see much of her on weekends."

Skyler looked at Hashim. "And I'll tell my grandmother than I'm sleeping over at Hashim's. We did that all through middle school. It's not a big deal."

Clarissa looked at Angel. "And I'll just say I'm spending the night with my sister and her kid. Are you sure you can make it?"

"Staying out all night will not be a problem." For once, his mother's problems actually worked in his favor. "She will never even know I'm gone."

Clarissa wasn't quite sure what Angel meant by that, especially with the way he said it, but it certainly sounded like he wouldn't have any problem getting away. "OK, tomorrow we'll go through the regular school day. Angel, do you have to work in the library after school on Fridays?"

"I'm only off when you guys have a game. It's not like I'm traveling with the team."

"Good. Because you have to be there. We want to help, but we're not going to do it all for you."

Hashim had done the math. "I figure you've been working there for two weeks. What are you doing? One hour a day?" Angel nodded. "So that's ten hours that you'll have by the end of this week. That means eighty hours left." He looked at Angel. "They must have given you all semester to do this." He looked at Angel. "Wow. That's like a regular job."

"Eighty hours left. Wow." Clarissa seemed to be the only one who fully grasped how long eighty or ninety hours were. "That is two full time forty-hour workweeks. If you had a job, that would be two weeks' pay." She looked at Angel. "What did you do?"

Hashim and Skyler gave Clarissa the same side-eye glance, "You shouldn't ask that!" look at the same time. Hashim continued his summary. "Anyway. Before I was interrupted." He looked back at Angel. "That leaves eighty hours. That's twenty hours for each of us."

Angel did not feel good about this. "I really appreciate it, but that's a lot of time. You don't have to do that."

"We may not do all of it," Hashim admitted. "But whatever we do, it will be four times more than you would have gotten if you did it yourself. We should be able to get at least twenty hours between the four of us. Maybe more. That's twenty hours you won't have to spend in there after school."

Angel felt good to be part of a team again, even if it was not the "team" he would have pictured a year ago. But he saw one critical flaw in the plan. "Roberts is my supervisor. As in "court-appointed supervisor. What if he decides not to sign for those hours? Technically, if he doesn't see me do it, then he can't say that I did it."

Clarissa had not considered the possibility that Roberts would not sign Angel's timesheet. She also didn't know how Roberts felt about whatever it was Angel had done to deserve such a sentence. She wasn't even sure if Roberts knew what Angel had done. But, if he did know, that might have a big part in how Roberts would feel about how his library was suddenly neat and orderly. Anyone who ever talked with Roberts or even just looked at him could tell that he wasn't real big on following the letter of the law. He was more of a "what was the intention behind this?" kind of person. But he was still a teacher. And, in Angel's case, he was working for the court.

Clarissa also knew that Roberts would do anything for his students. She was one of the few students who had figured out how many reeds, songs, and even instruments Roberts paid for out of his own money, and she suspected that even her estimate was probably low. Roberts never talked about that stuff. But Clarissa knew it happened.

Would Roberts be willing to lie for them?

"I guess that's a chance we'll have to take." Clarissa spoke slowly. "I don't know. The only thing that would stop him from doing it would be if he thought he would get in serious trouble for signing the timesheet when he didn't actually see the work get done." As she was saying that, Clarissa also realized that Roberts would have to ignore the fact that they had spent the night in the school. She was pretty sure that no one would check the security cameras as long as they didn't set off an alarm. Clarissa wasn't worried about getting caught like that. But would Roberts be willing to look the other way on this?

Clarissa realized she was going to have to talk to Roberts either before or after they finished in the library. She had to figure out whether it was better to get permission or to ask for forgiveness. She decided to keep those concerns to herself for the time being, although she was almost certain that Angel would have those same questions once he thought about it.

For the first time since she'd met him, Angel seemed happy. Skyler and Hashim were excited. Roberts would be happy just to have the room done.

Skyler and Hashim said their goodbyes and left Clarissa and Angel in the parking lot.

"I heard about what happened in weights and how you helped Skyler." Clarissa stopped walking and looked at Angel. "That was good."

"Coach didn't seem to think so. I'm sure he's questioning my masculinity as we speak, along with everyone else on the football team."

"That's stupid. People are stupid." Clarissa took a few steps and then stopped. "Standing up for an LGBTQ kid doesn't make you gay any more than defending animal rights makes you a dolphin."

"Then what does it make me?"

"A decent human being."

Clarissa kept going over their plan as she drove home. She decided that the possible risk was worth the potential reward. She also decided to accept whatever consequences might happen. She imagined what her own community service sentence might look like.

I'll probably get stuck working for Coach. Talk about Eighth Amendment issues.

23

Lunch Plans

Friday was game day at Hoag High School. The football team expressed solidarity with one another and with their Coach by wearing game jerseys to school. The cheerleaders exchanged their usual game-day attire of their slightly less than Saintly uniforms – all the same, yet some, somehow, so much less Saintly on some than others – for football jerseys as well. Those who had boyfriends wore their boyfriend's white travel jerseys, which struck Angel as odd since the team was wearing their home game blues to school and would need the white jerseys for the out of town game tonight. Ms. Carpenter also picked up on this little detail and warned the girls, "there'd better not be any jersey swapping in the parking lot." The cheerleaders who did not have a boyfriend on the team had all managed to get jerseys as well.

Clarissa, sporting her own "Saints Go Marching In" band shirt, watched the pairs of same numbered jerseys parading in the halls between classes. She wondered about the boys who were so desperate for the attention of a cheerleader that they would loan their jersey to a girl who wouldn't speak to them. Or the cheerleaders who were desperate to have a jersey.

"Everybody has a boyfriend on game day, even if it's pretend."

The Trio and Angel spent their morning sending and reading group text messages and thinking of ways to get into the band room after school. Clarissa did not see Angel in person until English class.

"The four of us should go somewhere for lunch and talk about this."

Angel liked the idea of going to lunch, but he wasn't sure how he felt about hanging out with The Trio where people might see them. Specifically, where the football team crowd might see them. Just because the team wasn't speaking *to* him did not mean that they weren't talking *about* him. He had heard whispers about him sitting with Skyler at the JV game and how he rescued her in weights. He couldn't prove it, but he wouldn't be surprised if Coach wasn't involved in some of that. Clarissa had a quick response when he had told her about it before English the other day.

"Were you planning on dating her?"

Angel remembered how surprised he was just by the question. "No."

"If you're not dating her, then what difference does it make?"

At the same time, Clarissa, Hashim, and Skyler were the only friends he had these days. They were not only friends. They were literally willing to work their butts off to help him. That's not just being a good friend. That's being a good person. He wasn't sure that any of his football friends would have done that for him, even when he was a part of the team. He knew that if the roles were reversed and it was Clarissa in the gym instead of him in the band room, he probably wouldn't have said anything to her, much less offer to help her the way they were volunteering to help him.

Clarissa repeated her idea. "So, what about it? Should we all go to lunch?"

Angel hesitated. "What about Hashim and Skyler? Ninth and tenth graders aren't allowed to leave campus for lunch." He thought about what was happening and how he felt about the people who were helping him. He wondered if band geeks felt about football players the way that football players were told they had to feel about band geeks. And what did it say about him that he even had a problem with this?

He looked at Clarissa and counted on his fingers as he spoke. "We're about to trespass on school property. Overnight. I am going to tell the judge that I worked the full ninety hours and in doing so, will commit perjury. And, to top it off, we're planning on asking a teacher to falsify court documents as part of a coverup." He smiled at Clarissa. "I don't think sneaking a couple of underclassmen off campus for lunch is going to be the real problem here."

"Yeah. I didn't either. You like Thai?"

"Thai sounds good." Text messages were sent. Lunch plans were made. Thai it was.

Angel had not been to the Thai place since the day he saw his mother there with the Cougar Hunter. He held the door open for the others to go in, not because he was polite but because it gave him a chance to look around the room and see if she was there. He wondered if it would be better to sit so he was facing away from the door, just in case she came in, or if he should face the entrance so he could see her if she did. He spent so much time looking around the restaurant that the decision was made for him when the other three took their seats without him. Angel faced the door.

Clarissa picked up a menu as Angel finally sat down. "Are you looking for someone?" Her eyes grew wide as she leaned across the table towards Angel. "Wait. Seriously. You're not like wearing an ankle bracelet or something, are you? Can you be here?" She looked around the room for undercover cops or secret government agents. "You know, it's not paranoia if they really are out to get you." Angel smiled and nodded appreciatively at her concern.

Hashim put down his menu. "He's doing community service, Clarissa. He's not under house arrest."

"Well, I don't know how these things work."

Angel scanned the room but tried not to be too obvious about it. He jumped when the waitress came up from behind him to take their order.

"Please put these all on one check," he said.

Clarissa did not want him to think this was a date, even if they were being chaperoned by Hashim and Skyler. "You don't have to do that."

"But I should. I just wanted to say thank you. All of you."

"Well, you're welcome."

Angel was trying to show Skyler how to use chopsticks for something other than drumming on the table when he heard the unmistakable sound of his mother laughing as she came through the door."

143

"That lady certainly seems happy," Clarissa's eye roll matched the inflection in her voice.

"Yeah," Angel said, looking at her and that man. "That would be my mother." His three lunch companions looked over the tops of their menus as she walked across the restaurant and took a seat at a table on the other side of the room.

"Oh. I'm so sorry. I didn't mean to say it like that."

"That's OK. That's pretty much how I've been saying it these days."

"Who is that with her?"

"I honestly have no idea." Angel realized how pathetic it sounded to not even know the name of his mother's boyfriend. "She seems to have a lot of friends."

"Oh." The tone of Clarissa's voice communicated much more than Angel had thought a single syllable word could convey."

"I didn't mean it like that," Angel said, although that is *exactly* how he meant it. "It's just that I don't know a lot of her friends."

"I don't think she saw you. Should you go say hello?"

"No." A short, yet unequivocal answer.

Clarissa understood. She didn't need to know the details. This wasn't some ridiculous cliché of a high school kid's fear of being embarrassed by his parents. Whatever this was, it was real. There was something there. That's all she needed to know.

"So, what's the plan?"

"Well, I thought we would all stay for practice like we always do anyway. Angel, you'll be in the library. I'll be on the stage. She pointed at Skyler and Hashim. "Are you two going to stay and practice?"

"I can," Skyler said.

"Was planning on it," said Hashim.

Clarissa continued. "I did find out that there will be some group in the gym, indoor soccer practice or something. So the front doors should be open until about 9:00." Clarissa did not point it out to Angel, but she noticed that his mom was already on her second lunchtime beer. She kept Angel distracted by looking at him while she talked. "So, let's leave around 5:30 like usual and then meet back at the school around 6:30. That will give everyone time to eat something and to do whatever they need to do before we get started."

"Works for me."

"Got it."

"Good."

Angel couldn't help flinching just a little every time he heard his mother laugh. He was just glad she hadn't seen him. Or, if she had, then he was grateful that she decided not to introduce herself to his new friends. He was trying not to look in her direction, but he couldn't help noticing that she and Cougar Hunter had their hands clasped on top of the table.

"Hashim, let me trade seats with you."

"Sure."

Angel spoke to Clarissa as he sat down next to her. "How do we get back in the band room? Wait. Don't you have a key?"

"No. Why would I have a key?" Clarissa looked shocked that Angel would even ask the question. "I'm the student conductor, not an assistant director. I don't have any privileges that you don't have."

Angel looked surprised. He knew that one of the managers for the football team, José, had his own key. Coach gave it to him so José wouldn't have to keep borrowing his. He had assumed that Clarissa was Roberts' version of José and probably had a key of her own, too.

Hashim did an exaggerated spit take with the water he was drinking. "Uh-huh. You're like his favorite."

"I am not." She thought about Roberts and his relationships with students. "He just likes people who love music as much as he does. I'm sure he feels the same way about both of you."

Angel wondered if this was going to turn into the kind of "You were always Daddy's favorite" argument that happened in the locker room. In that setting, he would have been the one saying, "No, I'm not." He didn't have to worry about that now. He wasn't really Coach's favorite, or at least it didn't feel that way at the time. Coach liked players who were good athletes, just like Roberts liked good musicians. Coach liked you even more if you scored points every game. The way their season was going this year, Angel guessed that Coach didn't like any of his players very much.

Skyler thought about it. "He seems to like all of his students, but he treats you differently if he thinks you're more serious about music. I wonder how people who treat band like a social club feel about how he treats them."

"With contempt bordering on disdain," Hashim said.

Clarissa looked at her phone and checked the time. "Guys, we don't have time for this."

Hashim finished up his spring roll. "I've stayed late to get ready for auditions and stuff. I've seen the janitor come in around 6:00. I always leave when he gets there. How long does it take to clean the band room?"

Clarissa looked at Hashim. "Could you go in there when he's there and hide in the library?"

Angel didn't think that would work. "Doesn't the janitor clean in the library?"

The Trio, in unison, looked at Angel. They did not need to say what they were thinking. Angel realized what the room they were talking about.

"Yeah. I guess not."

Hashim had another idea. "Instead of trying to catch the janitor with the door open, I'll just go in there and hide in the library while we're practicing after school. Roberts won't know. I'll text you guys when he leaves. You should probably wait a little before you come in, just in case he forgets something and comes back. You guys text me when you need me to open the door."

"Sounds like a plan." Angel took one last look at his mother. He turned back to Clarissa just in time to notice that Clarissa was doing the same.

"Let's get back. We can't be late for concert band and whatever it is you have fourth hour."

"Biology II. And I really don't care if I miss."

24

The Cleaning Crew

Roberts gave The Trio the usual "why are you late?" look as they came into concert band five minutes after class had started and the band was warming up. "Nice lunch, Hashim?" Hashim handed Roberts a fortune cookie as he passed behind the podium. "We're sorry. Have a cookie, Mr. Roberts."

Roberts suspected something was going on. His students only called him "Mr. Roberts" when they were in trouble.

His suspicions were renewed later in jazz band when he picked up on some conspiratorial looking glances between the members of the rhythm section. He dismissed those as just the way players look at each other when they're trying to anticipate what the other player is going to do. Rhythm players – all musicians, really – need to be able to communicate without speaking. He was glad to see that they were developing that skill. He wondered if, at this moment, it was being used for good or for evil.

Jazz band was really coming together nicely this year. Roberts thought it was a good sign that his rhythm section had started referring to themselves as "The Trio." It showed a certain pride in what they do.

They were a group within a group. His only complaint was that he wished Clarissa wasn't a senior. The band was always strong, but special groups like this don't come together every year. Roberts had learned to savor it when it happened.

Angel came in after school just like any other day. Roberts looked at the clock. "I hate to say this, but I really can't stay today. Sorry."

The Trio and its Plus One looked at each other. This was not part of the plan. Hashim made his way to the library while Clarissa made sure that Roberts was facing in the opposite direction. Angel closed the library door behind Hashim.

Roberts looked around the room to see that everything was put away. He walked towards the library. "Angel, how are you doing in here? Were you able to make any progress this week?"

"It's coming," he said. "Want to have a look?" Clarissa tried not to gasp as Angel opened the door and stepped into the library where Hashim was, hopefully, already hiding. Skyler almost panicked, but Angel seemed very confident in Hashim's ability to hide in the library until the janitor left. Then he would open the band room door to let them in.

Roberts stuck his head in the door for exactly long enough to say, "Looks good." Then he closed the library door without realizing he was leaving Hashim in the smaller room. "OK. Everybody out. I'll see everyone on Monday. Have a weekend!"

Clarissa smiled with relief. "Do you have special plans?"

Roberts' face showed his excitement for his plans. "I do! I am leaving here and going straight to Denver, where the lovely Mrs. Roberts and I will dine on meals in restaurants where you don't order by number.

Tomorrow we will admire the work of Monet in the Denver Art Museum, followed by more non-numeric dining on the international cuisine of our choosing, followed by our enjoying a new musical production of Sense and Sensibility at the Buell. We shall spend another luxurious night in our palatial hotel suite overlooking a beautiful city, followed by a stroll through the Botanical Gardens the next morning. And once the sun is high enough in the sky as to not be in my face as I drive home, we shall return."

"So basically, you're hanging out in Denver." Angel had a way of summarizing things in their most succinct manner.

It was 4:15. Hashim waited for the lights to go off in the main part of the band room. What was taking them so long to leave? Then he waited some more. Then he unfolded himself from the tornado drill seating position he was holding in the back corner of the library. He had thought about sitting behind the door when he came in but had decided to hide in the corner just in case. He was glad he was there and not behind the door when Roberts looked in.

There were no windows in the Mighty Marching Saints Band Room. There was outside light of any kind. The library didn't even have any exit lights like in the main room. Hashim didn't think he should turn on any lights before the janitor came by. That would be an invitation for the janitor to open the library door if he came into the band room. While he was reasonably sure that the library had not been cleaned in ages, he was not sure about whether the janitor would check the trashcan that was in the room. He still gagged when he remembered when someone tossed a half-full milk carton in the library trashcan last year. No one knew it was there until the entire room smelled like cheese. Not good cheese. Nasty cheese. It would be just his luck that he would be watching something on his phone, and the janitor would open the door and see him. It was going to be a long two hours.

The anticipated wait time became even longer when the janitor did not arrive as expected. By 6:45, Hashim's phone was blowing up with text messages from the other three asking if they could come in. The light in the main room came on just a little before 7:00. He expected to hear a vacuum. He did not expect to hear someone playing drums.

Whoever that is, they are really not very good.

He thought it might be Roberts, but this was bad even by Roberts standards. The Mystery Drummer was just trying to play a basic swing beat. The problem was he had no sense of swing. This had to be somebody who claps on one and three. The janitor certainly belonged to that demographic. Hashim's suspicions were confirmed when the drums stopped and he heard the vacuum. There were a few other sounds, then the light went off.

Hashim waited a few more minutes before he texted for the rest of the group to come in. Then he stood inside the door in the main room and waited to open it for the others.

The only team member who did not have a car was also the first team member to arrive. Skyler headed for the drums as soon as Hashim let her into the room.

"Who's been playing my drums?" She turned to Hashim, demanding an answer. "Did you play these?" The cymbals were out of place, the throne was the wrong height, and the toms were at a ridiculous angle. "My baby!"

"It was the janitor. And he really sucks."

Skyler snorted. "Probably claps on one and three."

Angel and Clarissa walked in together, a fact that did not go unnoticed by the drummer, no matter how upset she was about the condition of the drum set. Skyler wondered where that duet might end up, if not tonight, then sometime in the future Homecoming, maybe? Conspiracies have a way of making people grow closer.

Clarissa channeled her inner Leslie Knope and took charge. "OK… everyone over here. We need to figure out how to do this." Hashim was reasonably sure that "figure out" meant "listen to me," but that was not a bad thing. "The first thing we have to do is to keep track of Angel's time so we can honestly tell Roberts how many hours Angel put in." Clarissa had thought about what Angel said at lunch. She realized that it would be easier to get Roberts to keep quiet about them staying overnight in the school if she didn't also have to ask him to falsify Angel's timesheet. She looked at Angel. "We can help with the work, but we can't help with the hours. But, at least you won't be in there anymore. Maybe you can tune guitars or something."

She looked at the clock. "It is officially 7:36."

Angel knew nothing about tuning guitars, and he was afraid to ask what "or something" might mean in a band room. It didn't matter. The library was so overwhelming and so depressing that he did not care. Clarissa's plan also meant that he wouldn't have to lie about the total number of hours that he worked. He would still put in the full ninety. Plus, by working tonight for however long this ended up being, he would have to work fewer days, even if it was still the same number of hours. He felt much better about their chances of getting forgiveness since they hadn't asked for permission.

153

Meanwhile, Clarissa was showing significant project management potential. "I thought we could divide the music up into four groups and work from there. Hashim, do you want concert band, jazz band, pep band, or choir?"

"I am all about the jazz."

"OK. Got it. Skyler?"

"I'll do choir. That way, I can look at what they sing in there and decide if I want to join next semester."

Angel stroked an imaginary beard. "You know, singing was your first language." The Trio looked at him.

Clarissa raised her eyebrows and lowered her head. "Yeah. So I've heard."

25

Night Vision

"Seriously. Do you want pep band or concert band?" Clarissa looked at Angel. "If it doesn't matter to you, then I'll do concert. It will be like spending time with some old friends that I haven't seen in a while." She sighed and smiled. "That just makes me happy."

Skyler was shocked by the sheer mass of paper in the room. "How did this happen?"

Hashim knew exactly how it happened. "Think about it. There are 57 kids in the band. So, for every song, there are at least 57 pieces of loose paper floating around the room. So, there's that. Concert band usually does about, what? One new song a week? So that's nine songs each quarter, sometimes more, so let's say 10 times 57. That's at least 570 loose sheets of paper for every quarter. Multiply that by four quarters each year. There are at least 20 songs in the pep band folder. And about one song per week in jazz band, so that's a dozen parts for each of those. Plus, Roberts is terrible about pulling out music for the band to read only one time and then never putting it back."

Clarissa agreed. "Multiply that by however many years he's been here because he's never been great about putting things away. Then you have people who don't turn in their music until the end of the year or, like that one kid last year," Hashim and Clarissa looked at one another, smiled, and nodded, "when they graduate. That just gets thrown in here in random piles." She looked around the room. "Kaitlyn was working on reorganizing this two years ago. That was going to be her big thing before she graduated. That's why all these folders are all out of the file cabinets. I don't know what she was thinking. But then they had the COVID shut down so that all stopped."

Hashim remembered. "Remember when we were back in school and couldn't have band or choir at all? I hated that." He was right. COVID changed school music programs. At the very least, it stopped them from making any music for a while. Learning *about* music without actually *making* music is like learning to swim without water.

There was a spontaneous moment of silence as they remembered the lost year.

"Anyway, I'll do pep band. The little sheets. Got it." Angel headed towards the library.

"Wait!" Everyone stopped when Clarissa spoke. "We can't all fit in there. We're going to have to bring all that out here so we can sort it out and then put it away."

While Clarissa's plan was practical, it was not immediately popular with the other three. "You're basically doubling the workload," Hashim argued. "That's like digging a hole so you can fill in the same hole with the same dirt."

"Maybe." Clarissa was sticking to her guns on this. "But that room is small. And it's going to get smaller when we start leaving the file cabinet drawers open. I thought we could get the risers from the behind the stage and use those for shelves to help us sort things out."

Angel saw what she was trying to do. "Besides, if we do it that way, we'll be sorting it as we carry it out of the room instead of just moving piles around."

Everyone agreed that this was probably the best plan, even if it meant pulling all the music out only to carry it back into the library once it was sorted. "What happens if we don't get all this done tonight?" Skyler asked. "We can't just leave the risers out in the middle of the room with all that music on them." She laughed. "He might notice that."

Hashim had a thought. "We could gaslight Roberts and tell him that this is how he left it on Friday." More laughs.

Clarissa shook her head to say no. "Probably not. He can be forgetful, but he'd probably remember something like that. What we don't get done, we'll just have to put back in the library like it is."

They set up four sets of risers, one set for each type of music they would be sorting. They also cleared as much table space as possible and the top of the grand piano in case they needed that space. They didn't talk much, and when they did, it was barely above a whisper. There was just too much to do. It reminded Angel of the day he met Skyler and Hashim on the bleachers. Not much talk, but it felt good to be part of a team again.

Hashim was trying to pair his phone to the speakers in the band room. "We should put on some music!"

"NO!" Clarissa immediately lowered her tone. "Someone will hear it."

"Oh. Yeah. Didn't think of that. Ooops."

"Obviously not."

Angel was surprised how quickly everything moved once they got started. They went into the library one or two at a time, picked up a stack of their type of music, and carried it to their riser. Clarissa was arranging her music alphabetically by the first letter of the title. She even left gaps for the letters that didn't have any songs yet. The others noticed her system and did the same.

Clarissa left around 9:00 and returned with pizza and something to drink. "Break time!."

Angel looked at the clock. "The game is probably about over by now. I wonder how they did?" If the game was over by nine, then the team would be back around 10:30. "We'll probably hear them when they're putting away the balls and stuff."

Hashim took another slice of pizza. "Why do you have to do this anyway?"

Angel knew this was coming. They were helping him. It was natural they would want to know why. Did he really want to do this? He decided he might as well. "I accidentally bumped into a cop at the Black Lives Matter protest." He paused. "They frisked me. I had weed in my pocket."

Clarissa was surprised, but not shocked that an athlete would be arrested for weed. "You had weed?"

Hashim never got past the first part of Angel's confession. "You were at a Black Lives Matter protest?"

"It's not like it sounds. I mean, yeah, it's exactly how it sounds, I suppose. I was there. I didn't know it was a Black Lives Matter thing." He looked around their little circle for a pair of sympathetic eyes but found none. Their eyes had more questions than sympathy. "I didn't mean to go to the protest. I just saw a bunch of people and went over to see what was going on."

Hashim started to put his pizza down but stopped before he reached the table. He looked at Angel. "So, you were just slummin'?"

"Yeah." Angel was glad Hashim understood. "Just the wrong place, wrong time."

Hashim put his pizza on the table, his voice became more agitated. "More of a social justice tourist than any kind of social justice warrior." Hashim shook his head. "Another tourist."

Angel misinterpreted Hashim's resigned disappointment as a sign of sympathetic understanding of how he, Angel, had been so misunderstood and mistreated by the police.

"Exactly! I just wanted to see what was going on!"

Hashim stood up, slammed his fist into his own chest, and held it there. "I was what was going on!" Hashim inhaled deeply, then continued. "Me and about a hundred other people. That was my uncle you heard on the megaphone. My uncle was the big angry Black man that finally got your attention. And I was on those steps with him."

He leaned in towards Angel. "Do you support Black Lives Matter now?"

Angel struggled for what to say. "I don't pay attention to stuff like that. I know some people have been killed by the police. The police say they're just doing their job. I know something is wrong. I don't understand why people block streets and spray paint buildings."

"Then give me 8 minutes and 47 seconds and I will explain this to you." Hashim stood up, looked at his other two friends, and then locked in on Angel. "It's about Black people being killed by police!" Hashim stopped. He could not believe that he still had to explain this to people. What do they not get? "It's about acknowledging that Black people's lives matter just as much as anybody else's lives because clearly, they do not. White reporters always get it wrong. They say *Black* lives matter, with the emphasis on the *Black* part of it. They're trying to make it sound like Black people are saying that only Black lives matter and other lives don't matter at all. That is not what we are saying."

Hashim wanted to make sure Angel heard and understood what he was telling him. "That's not it at all. And when they do that, when they rebrand it like that, it's just an excuse for people to say '*All lives matter*' or '*Blue lives matter*' or any other name they want to put in there. Just slap it in there, insert your name here. They're appropriating it, just like they took blues, jazz, and rock and roll. And they don't even know what they're saying."

Skyler had not thought about which word was being stressed, but now that she thought about it, Hashim was right. She realized that she pronounced the phrase with an emphasis on Black. "It's just like where you put the accent on a measure full of eighth notes. They're all eighth notes, but that emphasis was the difference between a rock groove and the Norteña music that blared through her neighborhood on Saturday nights. Same thing here. She tried the sentence with an emphasis on each word. Clarissa also said the phrase with different inflections.

"*Black* lives matter. Black lives *MATTER*. Black *lives* Matter." It made a huge difference.

"How should they say it?"

Angel listened to Hashim. He had never seen anyone as angry about something as Hashim was about this, except maybe Coach. He realized that this was what the man with the megaphone was talking about.

Hashim was powerful. "If you ever heard a Black mother crying over her dead son, then you'd get it. Or a Black woman crying over her dead husband. Or a man crying over a dead Black woman, for that matter. They don't say *Black* lives matter when they're crying about someone they love. They say that this person's life *MATTERED*. This Black life *mattered.*"

He looked at Angel. "Those lives mattered to someone. That dead Black man was somebody's dad, somebody's son. Somebody's husband."

Hashim looked at Clarissa. "Somebody's mom."

Clarissa spoke up for the first time since Hashim started talking. "It's ridiculous that you have to remind people that those lives matter, too."

Hashim went on. " 'All lives matter.' Wow. Of course, all lives matter. But it's not *all* lives that are getting killed by the police. It's Black people, specifically Black people in the United States. If those Black lives mattered, they wouldn't be dead."

Clarissa looked at Angel. "You don't have to be Black to understand this. You just have to be human."

161

If the room had been quiet before, it was absolutely silent now. What do you say after that?

Angel had not thought about what Black Lives Matter actually meant to Black families or to a high school age Black guy like Hashim, who had probably been warned about being stopped by the police since he was in middle school. Maybe younger. He'd heard Black players on the team talking about "The Talk" that apparently all Black parents have with their teenage sons around the time they are in middle school. He couldn't imagine his mother warning him to watch out for the police even when he wasn't doing anything wrong or telling him what to do when, not if, he got pulled over.

Hashim must have read his mind. "When a White kid or a White parent says 'we had The Talk', they're talking about sex. The sex talk. When a Black kid says, 'we had The Talk', he's talking about the police. The how to stay alive talk."

Angel could certainly see how the phrase had been misread by newscasters and even by himself when he had seen it in print.

Again, silence. What can you say to that?

Clarissa still wanted to know more. "Just out of curiosity, what were the official charges? Assaulting an officer? Unlawful protest? Possession?"

Hashim spoke up before Angel could answer. "It was for possession, wasn't it? There were no other charges, right?"

"Yes." How did Hashim know that?

Hashim recognized the pattern. "Figures. The War on Drugs started when my grandmother was in high school. They couldn't arrest people for being Black. They couldn't arrest people for protesting the war. But they could arrest them for drugs. So they did. And when they saw how well that worked, they kept on doing it."

Clarissa was taken aback. "But drugs are bad, Hashim."

"Yes, Clarissa, drugs *are* bad. I'm not saying they're not bad. But they're also a convenient way to put people in jail, especially when you don't want them around in the first place. We blame doctors and drug companies for people getting addicted to opioids, but we throw crackheads in prison. You tell me the difference. There are entirely different penalties for drugs that White people use and drugs in Black communities." He looked at Angel. "You may have been charged with possession, but your crime was being at that rally. You just gave them an excuse to arrest you."

Again, silence. Hashim knew more about this stuff than anyone on the football team. Or maybe the football players knew better than to talk about it.

After a minute, Clarissa looked at the clock. "OK," she said slowly. "We need to get back to work." She looked at the visibly upset Hashim. "Hashim, you OK?"

"Yeah. I just get tired of having to explain this to people who should know better."

"I know." Clarissa hugged Hashim. After what seemed like a long time to Angel, Hashim pulled away. He just stood there.

Clarissa followed Angel into the library to get more music to sort. "Does Roberts know about why you are here?"

"Not unless the court told him. I didn't tell him. He said it didn't make any difference."

She smiled. "That's a very Mr. Roberts thing to say. So he doesn't know about the weed either?"

"No."

"That's probably a good thing. Both of his parents were alcoholics. And I think he has a brother who is an addict. Addiction and drug abuse are HUGE issues with him."

"So he would say that Hashim was wrong?"

Clarissa thought before she answered. "I don't think so. Roberts would probably say that this is a medical problem, not a crime. I know him pretty well. He's talked about his parents and his brother. He would say that addicts should be in treatment, not in jail."

"What about dealers?"

"No mercy. He has no sympathy for people who hurt other people. That's another big trigger for him."

Angel wondered if that was what Roberts was talking about when he said we stay in relationships until the pain of staying is greater than the fear of leaving someone behind. And about how trying to change them would change you. He was beginning to feel those same things about his own home.

Skyler joined Hashim and Clarissa in the library. Clarissa was more than a little claustrophobic. "Wow. Getting crowded in here!" She pushed Skyler out of her way and went back into the main room. Angel went over to Hashim.

"Sorry. I didn't mean…"

Hashim did not look up from the music he was sorting. "Whatever, man. It's all good." He shook his head as Angel walked away.

It was a little before 11:00 when they heard the sound of someone in the weight room next door. Angel recognized it as the sound of the football team returning from the game. He pointed to the light switch.

"Turn off the lights!" His voice sounded like a shout turned down to the volume of a whisper. The four of them sat by the door in the dark band room, waiting for the sounds and the voices to stop, trying to decide how long they should wait after the sound stopped.

"Maybe we should go in the library."

"No," Angel said. "They're talking in the hall right now. I want to hear what they say."

It was Coach and Coach Davis. This sounded like one of those conversations that start in one room and continue as you walk down the hall. They must have stopped somewhere near the band room door.

Coach Davis was clearly frustrated with the team and, possibly, even with Coach. "I understand all that, but we're not going to win any games this year unless we get Angel back on the team."

Coach was adamant. "And I'm telling you that I am not putting him back on the team. I don't care if he's a senior. I don't care if he's a good receiver. I don't even care if we never win another game. That kid is not putting that uniform on again."

"For weed, Coach? We're talking about weed here. I'm not saying it isn't serious. But he's missed three games now. And the courts already sentenced him to.. what? Ninety hours of community service? Something like that. I think he's working in the band room after school. He could probably reschedule and do that before school or on Saturdays."

Coach's voice became much louder and more aggressive. "You think this is about weed? This is not about weed. If we got rid of every kid who used weed, we wouldn't have an offensive line. This is about the other thing."

"What other thing?"

"The Black Lives Matters thing. I will not have one of our players embarrassing me or this school by going to some illegal protest rally. Especially not a protest for some radical leftist criminal group like Black Lives Matter."

"Really, Coach? Because we have a lot of Black kids on the team."

"And if they got arrested, I would do the same thing to them. People need to know that we mean business on this, just like we mean business on that taking a knee garbage. I am sick of these anarchists and their radical, violent protests. Those people need to learn who's in charge. They need to show some respect and appreciation for what they've been given here."

Coach searched for the words he wanted. "They need to be... broken." He looked Coach Davis in the eye like a drill sergeant. His voice growled. "This is our country, and we need to take it back."

Coach Davis had no idea how to respond to what he was hearing. He knew Coach had some strong feelings about players taking a knee when the band played the National Anthem. He had no idea that his objection to even peaceful demonstrations went this deep.

There had been no violence at the protests in Hoag. No riots, no looting, none of that. Some people with signs and a guy with a megaphone. These were just people who were upset and wanted to be a part of something bigger than themselves. They were regular people who had seen enough of people who look like them being killed. As peaceful disobedience goes, that rally at the courthouse was about as peaceful as it gets. The only thing more peaceful would be taking a knee at a football game.

The biggest problem with the protest in Hoag had been the car horns, revved engines, and loud exhaust pipes of the cars and trucks of people who were trying to shut down or, more precisely, shout down the demonstrators. Everyone said they objected to violent protests, with the emphasis on violence. Coach Davis understood that and even agreed that violence only made the situation worse. Hashim's uncle had been quoted in the newspaper saying that violence was counterproductive to what they hoped to accomplish. But it was pretty clear that for people like Coach, it wasn't the violence that bothered them. It was the fact that people would protest at all. When everything else was stripped away, it wasn't the violence that enraged people like Coach. It was the protest, the fact that someone would dare to disagree and challenge them and their idea of what is acceptable and what isn't.

Skyler and Angel couldn't believe what they were hearing. To Hashim and Clarissa, it was nothing new. Same speech, different speaker.

Coach's voice got louder and more emphatic. "They want to take down statues of our heroes. Can you believe that? Good men who fought for a cause they believed in, men who were willing to die for something they believed in. Who cares if they fought for the South! They were good, patriotic American heroes."

Coach Davis pondered the irony of Confederate soldiers being called "good patriotic Americans." He was a social studies teacher when he wasn't coaching the JV team or assisting on the Varsity. He was pretty sure that the men who went to war for the right to own slaves were not "good patriotic Americans." He didn't even think they qualified as good people, much less good Americans who should be memorialized in statues across the country.

"What's next? Are they going to force us to change our mascot because Saints is associated with Christianity? If they'll take down those statues, you can bet they'll be coming after Christians next!"

"Wow," thought Coach Davis. "Coach, I don't think you can compare removing Confederate memorials to erasing Christianity."

The voices in the hall got softer as the men walked away. The lights in the hallway went off.

They sat in silence as what they had just heard sank in. Clarissa searched for any excuse to talk about something else. "Huh. I've been here four years, and I did not know those lights could be turned off." It was a shallow comment, totally unlike anything Clarissa would usually say. She immediately regretted saying it. But she was that desperate to break the tension.

"I've been here four years, and I didn't know Coach was … whatever that was," Angel said. He looked at Hashim. "That was pretty messed up. Comparing Confederate soldiers to Jesus."

Hashim had heard enough. "I'm going home. Hopefully, I won't be shot for walking while Black."

Angel looked at the clock. It was 11:17. With the dinner break and this, he'd only gotten in about four hours of work, not nearly as much as he had hoped. Still, that was four hours he wouldn't have to work after school, assuming Roberts went along with all of this. Between the four of them, it was 16 hours less time in the library. At least. He was pretty sure that their hours of sorting music were more productive than his hours would ever be.

Clarissa caught up to Hashim in the hall. "I'll give you a ride. Wait up." She was also disappointed that they hadn't done more, even though she completely understood why Hashim needed to leave. There was also the problem of the risers and all that music spread out across the band room. She did not want that to be the first thing Roberts saw when he came in on Monday. She pulled Angel away from the others.

"Could we work on this tomorrow?"

Angel wondered what she had in mind. "How would that even work?"

"The building will be open tomorrow for something. It always is. All we have to do is get back in this room." She paused. "Let's just prop the band room door open so we can get back in."

"What if Roberts comes back tomorrow sometime?"

"Then we'll deal with that when it happens. I'll deal with it." Clarissa was concerned about Hashim and how he had reacted to Coach's rant. It's one thing to know those attitudes are out there. It's something else when you see them in your school, right in your face. It's even worse when you see those attitudes in people with power and influence. Like Coach.

"Everybody go home. Hashim, you and Skyler can ride with me."

Angel looked at The Trio. Then he looked at Hashim. "I am so sorry."

"I know. It's not you. It's just everything."

26

By the Dawn's Early Light

Angel drove home wondering whether Coach said the Pledge of Allegiance to the Stars and Stripes flag of the United States or the crossed bars flag of the Confederacy of the Civil War. Obviously, he said the Pledge of Allegiance every morning along with the rest of the school. But which flag represented the "America" for which Coach stood?

They may have been hiding in the dark, but the conversation they overheard made some things very clear. Like how Coach let some of the guys on the team wear jackets and baseball caps with the Confederate flag on them while other teachers would not allow it in their classroom. Coach started talking about "protecting our heritage" at the end of the season last year. Angel had assumed he was talking about a football legacy, winning the championship, something they ultimately did not do. Stuff like that. Now Angel wasn't so sure. Was there some secret code with secret words and hand signals that no one told him about?

Angel walked into an empty house. No sign that Mom had been there at all. He thought about texting The Trio but decided it was too late. Besides, Hashim didn't look like he felt like talking to anyone when they were leaving. It was probably best to just leave everyone alone and let them get some sleep.

Hopefully, they were sleeping better than he was these days. When did everything get so crazy?

He thought about tomorrow, which was rapidly becoming later on today, and how they might get into the building. The Varsity game was away, which meant the JV would be at home tomorrow for a 1:00 game. The JV players, or at least the managers, would show up at the school by 11:30 to start getting ready. He and The Trio could go in then, but it would be nice if they could get in earlier and finish up what they had started, or at least get everything put away so Roberts wouldn't see what was going on before they were finished.

After the whole Black Lives Matter conversation and Coach's rant outside the band room door, Angel wasn't even sure if Hashim would show up at all. Angel didn't think Hashim was angry at him specifically, although he was clearly frustrated with having to explain why Black Lives Matters, well, *mattered*. It was more like he was just tired of the entire thing. Tired of seeing pictures and videos of people who look like him getting shot or choked by police. Tired of seeing privileged Karens calling the police because Black kids were playing in the park. Tired of having to explain why Black people might be upset by four hundred years of that.

And really tired of haters like Coach.

Coach. *How did I miss that?* It's amazing what you don't see when you aren't looking for it. When you don't think to look for it. When you don't want to look for it.

Angel wondered what else he had missed because he didn't want to look for it. Like Mom. How long had she been missing work? He knew when she started spending the night away from home. That was a recent development, at least the overnight part of it. But how long had she been seeing this guy? How many days had she missed work because she thought it was still the weekend?

He got a group text around 12:30.

Clarissa: There's some little kid basketball thing going on in the gym tomorrow. Starts at 8:00. Want to meet at the school then?

Skyler: Sure. Can you give me a ride?

Clarissa: Yes. Angel, can you be there?

Angel didn't feel like texting a reply, so he just went with one of the auto-generated responses that appeared on his screen.

Angel: I'll see you then!

He wouldn't have chosen the exclamation point. The predicted text was just a little too perky, especially with how the night had ended. But it was one less thing he had to think about. Just tap and go.

There was a long pause. Angel wondered if Hashim was asleep or just angry. He questioned if Hashim would even come back tomorrow. He hoped that Hashim didn't think of him as only a younger version of Coach.

His phone finally buzzed.

Hashim: I'll be there.

This time, the suggested auto replies were fine, but Angel felt like he should type this one out by hand. He didn't know why. It just seemed like that was the right thing to do.

Angel: Thank you.

Somehow it just felt more human, more respectful, even if, to the reader, it was all the same.

He eventually fell asleep sometime after 1:00AM. As always, he was awake by 6:00. He rarely got more than four or five hours of sleep anymore. He checked his phone. No new messages. He checked Mom's bedroom. Nothing new there either.

At least The Trio was there for him, even if nobody else seemed to be.

Angel got to school by 8:00. The front doors were open, just like Clarissa said they'd be. He thought about waiting for the others before he went in, but decided he would show them his gratitude by being the first one there.

He discovered he was the last one to arrive.

"Sorry. I thought you said it was open at 8:00."

"They opened a little earlier. We were already here, so we came in." Clarissa looked around the room, easily her favorite place in the school. It was certainly the safest room for people like Hashim and Skyler. And her. And for anyone who struggled with the prevailing culture of Hoag High School or the world in general. She hoped Angel wouldn't change the feelings she had for this room by dragging that culture into here.

"Let's get to work."

They picked up where they left off the night before, carrying music from the library and sorting it on the risers. The JV team arrived at 11:30, right on schedule. They could tell by the loud music coming from the locker room. And then it was quiet again.

Clarissa left to get lunch around 12:30. When she returned, they ate in the library, on the cleared table that at this time yesterday had been covered in music. They had moved so much paper and so many boxes that they could actually fit four chairs around the table.

Angel looked around the library and then at each member of The Trio. "Thank you. Seriously. I was dying in here. You guys saved me. Thank you."

"You're welcome."

"Sure."

Hashim was the last to speak.

"It's what we do." Fist bump with Skyler.

While they were eating, Clarissa explained how the music was supposed to be filed away and which file cabinets were dedicated to which groups. They weren't ready for that part of the process yet, but they were getting close. By a little after 3:00, they were ready to start putting music in the correct file cabinet drawers, neatly organized by which band or choir played those songs and in alphabetical order by composer. Except for pep band. That was alphabetized by the names of the songs. Clarissa always thought it was sad that nobody cares who writes a pop song.

Finally, around 6:00 that evening, the last folder was put in the file cabinets. The risers were taken to the stage.

"I've been here three years, and I have never seen this room look like this." To say Clarissa was happy would be an understatement. "This is awesome!"

Hashim was also impressed. "I didn't think this could happen." Fist bump.

Skyler was excited and was not ready to leave. "We might as well organize the percussion closet next." She opened the door to where the percussion equipment was kept, along with amps and other miscellaneous things. The percussion closet was another Chamber of Horrors. No one else thought that was a good idea. Percussion could wait. Angel could do that with the hours he had left.

Angel felt a sense of accomplishment that he knew he didn't deserve. "Thank you. All of you. I don't even know what to say."

Hashim put their cups and the pizza box in the trashcan. "You might want to figure out what to say when Roberts comes in here on Monday."

Clarissa looked at Angel. "I'll talk to Roberts. Let me do that." She looked around the room, then at Angel. "What are you going to do with the rest of the hours?"

"Don't know. I'll see what Roberts says." Angel had kept track. By his count, he had worked 14 hours, with one hour off for lunch. He wasn't sure what to do about the time they spent listening to Coach last night. He decided to err on the side of honesty. He looked at Clarissa.

"So, 12 hours for my work time?"

"That sounds about right. I'll tell Roberts that you worked 12 hours and that we helped."

Angel did the math. "That's 48 hours of work time between the four of us." More than that, really. Angel knew that their hours were much more productive than his hours would have been if he had done this alone. He could not imagine ever finishing this without their help.

27

Date Night

Clarissa dropped Hashim and Skyler at Hashim's house and then headed home. Angel went back to an empty house with no sign that his mother had been there. He thought about texting her to see if she'd reply, but decided against it. Why bother?

Instead, he texted Clarissa.

Angel: Feel like Thai? Send. Wait for the response.

Wait some more.

And some more.

Finally, Clarissa replied: *Not really.*

"Fail. Good job, Angel." Angel put his phone down on the kitchen table. "She thinks I'm a football player, so I must be like Coach," he said to the empty chair across the table. He got a burrito from the freezer and put it in the microwave. *Why would she — they — help if they thought I'm just another hater?* And why would they come back this morning? "They probably didn't trust me to put things back." Forgiveness may be easier than permission, but it would be easier to ask for forgiveness if there wasn't music all over the band room when Roberts walked in Monday morning.

His phone buzzed again.

It was a text from Clarissa:

But Cocina Veracruz sounds good.

Angel replied right away:

Yes it does.

He actually had no idea if Cocina Veracruz sounded good or not. It sounded Mexican. That was as much as he could tell. He'd never been there. His mother was a Mexican food snob. Angel could not remember the last time they went to a Mexican place. When he would ask his Mom if they could go to a Mexican restaurant, her usual response was "Ay frijoles y tortillas en la casa." It was one of the few times she spoke Spanish in their home. Angel was not fluent in his mother's native language. On the rare occasions when she could be persuaded to go to a Mexican place, it was "¡Tu Abuela *nunca* comería esto!," which just sounded so much snarkier than the English translation, "Your grandmother would never eat this!," could ever hope to sound, probably because of the extra upside-down exclamation mark that Spanish speakers used. He laughed when he remembered telling her "¡Mi Abuela no esta aqui!," which he thought was funny but which proved to be the wrong thing to say to his Mexican mother. And then she ordered a margarita. So much for talking with Mom in Spanish.

"That's probably when she started drinking, right there." Angel's sense of humor had taken a decidedly dark turn as of late.

179

Clarissa texted back:

I'll tell Hashim and Skyler.

The suggested text response on Angel's phone needed no adjusting.

No.

"Big yikes," Clarissa said out loud as she put her phone down. She was OK with having dinner with Angel, but this was looking like he was asking her out on a date. She did not want to start dating this guy. He seemed almost as desperate as those guys on the football team who got suckered into loaning their game jerseys to some cheerleader who couldn't care less whose jersey she had on. *Everybody has a girlfriend on game day.*

She didn't want a date, but she did want to see where this would go:

Why not?

"Why not? What kind of question is that?" After Angel thought about it, he knew exactly what kind of question it was. She was either stalling because she wasn't sure, or she was just messing with him at this point. He wasn't as upset about the question as he was with himself for not anticipating it and having a response ready to go. He had to think fast.

You just did me a huge favor. The least I can do is buy you dinner.

Of course, Skyler and Hashim had also done him a huge favor, and he wasn't offering to take them out to eat. Hopefully, Clarissa won't overthink this.

Long wait. *This woman is either the slowest texter ever, or she really thinks about what she is about to say.*

180

His phone finally buzzed.

OK

Score! His confidence restored, Angel decided to go for the extra point.

Tell me where you live and I'll pick you up.

Yeah. Hard pass on that. Clarissa smiled. But she was impressed that he would take her to Cocina Veracruz. She had thrown that name out because she didn't think Angel would go. It was a test, and Angel passed it. Cocina Veracruz was nicer than the Thai place and not cheap. Not many high school boys would take someone there, especially for a casual dinner. She also realized that she may have unintentionally changed Angel's original plan when she told him she wanted to go to the Cocina. Dinner for four could be pretty expensive at a place like that.

I'll just meet you there. Give me about 45 minutes.

Angel was disappointed but also somewhat relieved. He had no idea where this place was or anything about it. He would have to get directions to get there, and he didn't want his phone screaming directions at him while Clarissa was in the car. That is not part of the mature image he wished to convey. Even worse, he did not want to have to ask Clarissa how to get there. He may not be picking her up, but he also wasn't looking like a dork, either.

I'm going out with a band geek, and I'm worried about looking like a dork. Wow.

Clarissa decided that even though this wasn't a date, she wanted to wear something a little different than what she wore to school every day.

She looked at the black dress she wore for band concerts, the one she'd bought the first year she made All-State. She loved that dress. It was full of good memories, but it also just looked good. Above all, the black dress was comfortable. She spent what little extra time she had on her makeup and "borrowed" her mother's pearls for the final touch. Then she twisted her hair up the way that only women with long curly hair can do. She was ready to go.

Angel managed to find his way there, thanks to the help of Google Maps. He was pretty sure that Clarissa was already there, so he went inside. He immediately felt underdressed. It wasn't that he looked *bad*, really. At least he had put on a clean shirt. But he was definitely on the lower end of the acceptable wardrobe spectrum for this establishment. Oh well. Too late now.

Clarissa was not there yet, or at least the hostess didn't think she had seen anyone that matched Angel's description of her. The hostess said it should be about a fifteen-minute wait for a table. Angel took a seat.

His phone buzzed. It was Clarissa.

I'm here. Should I wait for you inside?

Angel texted back right away.

I'm already inside.

He saw her as soon as she walked through the door. Clarissa looked amazing. Angel had taken girls to prom and had been to other dress-up events. But prom dresses aren't really classy. Prom dresses are just a high school girl's idea of classy, which, he always suspected, was based on what they thought was a high school boy's idea of what was classy. Clarissa, in her black dress and pearls, was none of that. She was the real

182

thing, not some badly-drawn caricature of a woman that was as fake as the cheap cardboard backdrops and pretend wine glasses they had at prom.

He did not know what to say, so he went with "Nice dress." Can't lose with a compliment to the wardrobe.

Clarissa smiled. "Thank you." She started to add that it was the dress she wore for concerts but decided against it.

They were seated and presented with menus. The hostess asked if either of them were over 21 and then removed the wine glasses when they both said they weren't.

"We could have lied," Clarissa said. "But we probably wouldn't have gotten away with it."

Angel looked at his not-date date. "You could have easily gotten away with that with how you look." Clarissa smiled but pulled the menu up so Angel wouldn't notice.

Angel opened his menu and looked for something familiar. "Wow. This is, like, all seafood."

"It's Cocina Veracruz. What did you expect?"

He had not expected an upscale Mexican version of Red Lobster. He was glad he'd brought the credit card that his mom let him use for gas and stuff. Food qualified as "and stuff," right?

Clarissa laughed. "The name literally means 'A Kitchen in Veracruz.' And Veracruz is all about shrimp and fish." She rolled her brown eyes. Angel noticed the way her hair moved when she shook her head. "And that's about *all* I got out of Señor Medina's Spanish class."

"Right," he said. "Ay frijoles y tortillas en la casa." Clarissa looked puzzled and wished she could remember more from Spanish class, or that she had been taught more. She was pretty sure Angel was saying something about having beans and tortillas at the house. Angel saw the concentration on Clarissa's face. "It's just something my mom says."

"You speak Spanish?"

"No. My mom does. But my dad does not, so she never spoke it when he was there." He looked around the room. "Unless we were going to a Mexican restaurant. It's a Mexican Mom thing."

"I see." Clarissa went back to ruling out menu items according to price. She flipped the menu over. "If you don't like seafood, there are other things on the last page." *OMG. There's a hamburger.* She looked at Angel and smiled as she thought to herself. "*Please don't be the kind of person who comes to a place like this and orders a hamburger.*"

"No, no. I am all in." He'd come this far. He was not going to wimp out now.

"Good! I am starving." *Good. He's not that person.*

Angel took a sip of water and looked for something familiar. Would she think he was cheap if he ordered the fish tacos for fifteen bucks? That seemed like a reasonable compromise for someone who eats fish like, what, once a year? He was glad she hadn't suggested sushi.

28

The Order

Clarissa closed the menu. "I am going to get my favorite, the salmon tacos." Angel took a quick glance and the price and silently cheered at how she had unknowingly given him permission to also order from the lower-priced end of the menu. That could have been a lot worse.

"Thank you for bringing me here."

"Thank you for helping me in the library."

"You're welcome."

They said nothing, but they both had the same thought at almost the same time.

"Yeah. That's all I got. I hope he/she can think of something to talk about."

The awkward silence was broken when their server came to take their order.

Clarissa decided to be brave and go first. "Did your mom say anything when you came in last night?"

"No. Not really." *Of course, she didn't. She wasn't home.*

Clarissa picked up one of the few tortilla chips that remained in the basket. "My parents were already asleep. This morning they asked why I hadn't spent the night with my sister like I told them I was going to." She paused and laughed a little. "I had forgotten I had told them that. I just told them that I decided I wanted to sleep in my own bed."

"Good answer. It's the quick responses like that that really make the difference in times of crisis."

Clarissa laughed. *That's good,* Angel thought. *She laughed at a joke that really wasn't that funny. This is going well.*

Angel munched on chips to fill in the gaps in the conversation. He didn't realize that he had managed to eat almost the entire basket of chips by himself until he got down to just the last few. "I'm sorry. I didn't know I had so many of those."

"It's OK. I'm saving room for the tacos."

Angel was trying to think of something, anything, to say. It wasn't like he could talk about the football team or the big game or any of his usual go-to topics, most of which, he was now realizing, centered primarily around himself. Once again, it was Clarissa to the rescue.

"What did your mom say when you told her we were going out for dinner?"

Angel thought about his answer and was glad that, once again, he would not have to lie. "Not much. She didn't really say anything."

"That's the difference between girls and boys, I guess." Clarissa sighed. "Oh well. I guess a double standard is better than no standards at all, right?"

"Right." *Was I supposed to laugh at that? Crap.*

"My parents wanted to know everything, starting with why I hadn't told them sooner that we were going to dinner. Then they wanted to know about you."

"What did you tell them?"

"That you were a nice boy who got arrested for having weed after you assaulted a cop at a Black Lives Matters protest."

Angel tried not to look shocked. "Well, yeah... Glad you gave them a positive impression."

She looked at his brown eyes. "They were very impressed."

"As they should be." Angel hoped the food would come to his rescue soon, even if he wasn't that hungry.

Clarissa laughed. "Just kidding. I would never tell them that. But they did want to know about you. I just told them that I met you in the band room. That seemed to be OK with that."

"Because band kids are so well behaved?"

Clarissa laughed again, even louder than before. "You don't know very many band kids, do you?"

Their demeanor became more relaxed once their meals arrived, smoothed over by the tacos that provided cover for any awkward silences in the conversation. Clarissa talked about how she had wanted to be a band director since middle school. "I wanted that even before I met Mr. Roberts. I think that's why we got along so well right away. Being in his band just made me want it more." She talked about her upcoming auditions, honor bands, scholarships, and different groups she had played with around the state. She talked about how much music meant to her.

She leaned forward and whispered. "There's this thing we say in the band room, one of those things that are supposed to stay in the band room."

"Why do I feel like there are a lot of those things that are supposed to stay in the band room?"

"Because there are. We say, 'They are *on* the team. We are *in* the band.'"

He was beginning to understand her commitment to music. She was just like he was with football. It was the same drive, just different ways of letting it out.

"How much do you practice every day?"

"You mean by myself?" She thought about it. "On school days, it's about two hours, maybe a little more. One hour in the band room after school and another later at night when I'm home."

Angel put his taco back on his plate. "You practice two hours a day by yourself? Not counting what you do in band?"

She just nodded her head and tried not to laugh with food in her mouth.

Angel felt bad for asking her when she had just taken a bite. "Sorry. I'm practicing for a career as a waiter."

"At least. Sometimes more. Definitely more on weekends. Last year, before All-State, I was up to about four hours a day by myself. I would ask Señor Medina if I could go to the band room instead of Spanish. Roberts let me practice on the stage."

"That's probably why you never learned any Spanish."

"Yeah. We'll go with that."

The more they talked, the more Angel wanted to tell her why his mother didn't ask about his dinner plans. He'd been carrying a lot of stuff inside lately. It would be nice to tell somebody what was going on in his life, just how crazy everything had become. Last night was the first time he'd said anything to anyone about why he was arrested. He missed being on the football team even more than he thought he would. He missed his friends on the team. And he hadn't told anyone about what was going on with his mom, although he assumed that Clarissa had some idea after seeing her at the Thai place.

Hey, I could talk about that. "I wonder if Thai parents feel the same way about Thai restaurants that my mother feels about Mexican places." He looked around the nicely decorated room. "Although she might like this place. We never went anywhere like this."

Clarissa thought about it. "They might, just like Italian parents might feel that way about Olive Garden."

"Everybody feels that way about Olive Garden." Angel noted that Clarissa only sort of laughed at that joke, but it wasn't much of a laugh. Maybe she really liked Olive Garden, and he had just insulted her. *That was an unforced error — loss of one point.*

He was on his second taco and she was still on her first when he decided he wanted to tell her about his mom. It took him the rest of the taco, eaten very slowly, to figure out how he wanted to break that news.

189

"My mom's been spending nights out a lot lately. I don't know what's going on there."

"She's dating somebody." Clarissa shrugged her shoulders and was very nonchalant about the whole thing. "That's what people do when they're divorced. They date other people."

"Not like that. I mean, yeah, there's some guy."

"That guy she was with at lunch?"

"Yeah."

"Wow. Young."

"Thank you! Yes!" Angel was glad he wasn't the only one who thought he was too young for her. He felt vindicated but not relieved.

Clarissa put the taco back on her plate without taking another bite. "But, if it was reversed… I mean, if your dad was dating a woman who was that much younger than he is, everybody would think he was a stud." She took a sip of water. "It's that whole double standard thing again."

"Yeah." Angel didn't realize he was raising his glass to his lips at the same time she was until the water hit his mouth. He swallowed and tried not to think about what that might mean. "But, if it was my dad and he was dating a woman that much younger, she would be a babe. This guy's not… whatever it is that is the male equivalent of that. He is not a boy babe."

"The term you're groping for is 'boy toy.'" Clarissa put her hand to her mouth and laughed. "Sorry. 'Groping' was probably not the word you wanted to hear concerning some guy dating your mother. And, yes, your mother is dating a boy toy." She put her hand back on the table. "He's kinda hot, actually."

"Are you kidding me?"

She did her best "I don't know…" expression and held it for as long as she could without being overly cruel. Then she broke character. "No. He's a creeper." She returned her napkin to her lap and looked down as she smoothed out the creases. Then she looked back at Angel. "Does that make you feel any better?" Without realizing it, she reached her hand across the table toward his, close but not touching. "So, she's having a sleepover with some guy. I could see how that could bother you, but it is her life. She's a grown woman."

"She's also drinking a lot more. Like, a *lot* more. For lunch, in the evenings, that is, when she's home. I think she's even drinking wine before she leaves for work. I woke her up on Monday so she could get ready for work, and she told me she didn't work on Sundays. She had missed an entire day."

"That's not good. I'm sorry to hear that."

Angel decided that was enough sharing for one night. He finished his third and final taco. Clarissa finished her second and said she was full. The server brought the check, Angel pulled out his credit card, and they headed for the door.

Angel walked Clarissa to her car. "Look," she said. "If you ever need to talk or something, let me know. Seriously. It sounds like you're going through a lot right now. Let me know if I can help."

"Thanks. That means a lot."

"I had a good time tonight. Thanks for asking."

"Thanks for saying yes."

29

Goodnight

Angel didn't hear from Clarissa, his mother, or anyone else all day Sunday. He spent the day playing Overwatch and trying to find somewhere that sold fish tacos for less than $5 each. His phone was silent until around 9:00 that night when he got a text from Clarissa.

Clarissa: We should probably get to school early tomorrow morning so we can beat Roberts to the band room and go in with him.

"Good point." He tapped out his reply.

Angel: When does he usually get there?

Clarissa: I don't know. Had kids coming in last week at 6:30. Don't know if that's every morning.

Angel: 6:30? Really?

Clarissa: Really. It may be different tomorrow.

Angel: We should be there. Weightlifters come in at 6:00. Use those doors to get in.

Clarissa: OK. See you around 6:15?

Angel: Sounds good. Goodnight, Clarissa.

Clarissa: Goodnight, Angel.

Angel listened for the door to open. He waited for her laugh, her voice, her presence.

Just to know she was home. He set his alarm to wake up at 5:30.

He kept waiting.

Then he fell asleep.

30

Clean One Mess, Create Another

Angel was already awake when his alarm went off at 5:30. He knew that would happen when he was setting the alarm the night before, but he did it anyway. It was more like a reminder to get out of bed than it was to wake him up. She didn't usually wake up before 6:00 if she was even at home. He knocked on her closed bedroom door, quietly at first, then louder. He pushed the door open just a crack and saw the unused bed. There was no need to step into her bedroom.

His first thought was that he should leave the door open so she would know he had checked on her. He even thought about messing up the bed, so it would look like she had slept in it. That would mess her up, some more "what did I miss?" stuff. Then he wondered if she would even notice it or think about it at all. Probably not.

He checked his phone. No messages from her.

He drove to school and parked next to Clarissa's car. They walked to the door that the weight lifters use for their early morning lifting. They had to go through the weight room to get to the hall and the band room. Coach glared at Angel as he walked past, but he didn't say anything.

They stepped into the hall. Roberts was standing in front of the band room door.

Clarissa waved. "Good morning, Mr. Roberts!"

Funny how they call me Mr. when there's a problem.

Roberts waited for them to walk to the door. "How was your weekend?" Clarissa asked.

"My weekend was great, Clarissa. How was yours?"

Angel didn't know what was happening here, but this felt weird. Roberts had this weird, Jack Nicholson smile thing going on. He looked at Clarissa to see if she might show any sign that she felt the same thing that he felt. If she did, she was doing an excellent job of covering it.

Roberts dug into his pocket to find his keys. "My weekend was good, thank you." He jiggled the key but did not open the door. "It got really interesting when I came up here yesterday." He looked at both of them. "Ran into Coach." He looked at Angel. "He's an interesting man, isn't he?"

"He can be."

"Fascinating man. He wanted to make sure that the band was going to keep on playing *"When The Saints Go Marching In"* when the team ran onto the field. I'm not sure why he's suddenly so concerned about that. Weird." Roberts opened the door and looked back at them.

"Come on in." Clarissa and Angel looked at one another but said nothing.

"But that was not the strangest part of my weekend," Roberts said.

Clarissa knew where this was going. "I bet not."

"Yeah. So, anyway, I came up here last night. I open the door, walk in here, and the first thing I notice is four drink cups in the trashcan. Not a big deal. Sometimes the janitor misses things, but I think I would remember letting four people have drinks in my beverage-free band room. Sometimes I even leave pizza boxes in the trashcan, like that one over there, the one that almost fits in the trashcan."

He opened the door to the library.

"But, I have never left the library looking like this." The library was immaculate. Angel and Clarissa were so tired when they left Saturday that they had not fully appreciated what the four of them had accomplished. They were proud. And scared. Pride mixed with fear. Mostly fear.

"This... " he looked around at the straightened shelves, the clear tops of the file cabinets, the uncluttered floor. "This is amazing." He turned to the two guilty-looking students. "And it probably represents the violation of all kinds of school policies about unsupervised students in the building after hours and at least a couple of state and local laws." He looked back at the shelves. "But it is no less amazing. I am impressed."

He looked at Clarissa and Angel. "Do either of you want to tell me what happened here?"

Clarissa was the first to speak. "We wanted to do something nice for you."

"Right. So this is for me. Why do I think there's more to this?"

It was Angel's turn to speak. "This was all my idea. Clarissa and I hid in the library after school on Friday. We came out after the janitor cleaned the room." He looked at Clarissa and then back at Roberts. "The janitor is a horrible, horrible drummer. You are much better."

"Be that as it may." Roberts turned to Angel. "Really bad, huh? Like he really sucks? Cause he talks like he's some kind of great drummer."

Angel continued. "He's seriously horrible."

Clarissa chimed in. "Like a pair of shoes in a dryer. I was embarrassed for him." She hoped Roberts didn't ask for details.

"Hmm... Well, be that as it may, would either of you like to try that story again? There is no way just the two of you cleaned this room in a few hours on Friday night." He pointed to the trashcan. "There are four drink cups. Two of them have lipstick on them. Different shades of lipstick, which kind of makes me think they're from different people."

Roberts looked at Angel. "I'm not sure I can say 'Don't tell me, doesn't matter' on this one." Angel remembered the first time he heard Roberts say that. It was when he was asking Roberts about working in the band room.

He picked up one of the incriminating cups. "I'm going to guess this isn't Rachel's."

Rachel? Who's Rachel? Angel didn't know any Rachel.

Clarissa cleared her throat. "It's Skyler's."

Roberts picked up the other cup. "Hashim?"

"Yes."

"How did I know that?" Roberts looked at the clock. School wouldn't start for another thirty minutes.

"I am torn here. On the one hand, I am extremely grateful. Thank you for cleaning the library. Seriously. I have never seen this room look like this. I may cry. After you leave, of course. Not in front of you. And if you ask later, I will deny having said that."

"You're welcome." Clarissa really was happy to see that he was so pleased. She knew how much the mess in the library bothered him.

Angel was waiting for the other shoe to drop.

"On the other hand, what am I supposed to do? What happens to me if I don't report this? What if somebody saw you and they report it?"

Roberts looked at Clarissa. "Why did you really do this?"

Angel spoke up instead. "Like Clarissa said, we knew it bothered you…"

Clarissa shook her head and then looked at Angel. "Stop." She turned to Roberts. "This was my idea. Angel was dying in here. He was not going to get it finished in ninety hours or ninety years. And," she looked at Angel "he's going through a lot right now, with the team, and this…" she corrected herself "…that mess, and.."

Angel looked at Clarissa. His eyes said, "please don't."

Clarissa saw Angel's expression and adjusted her course. "And all that. I thought we could help him and help you at the same time. Everybody wins."

"Clarissa, this conversation would be very different if this were any student other than you. I think you know that. And I think that is part of the reason that you thought I would be OK with this." He kept looking around the freshly organized former disaster. "That part is my fault, for treating you like an assistant director, for thinking of you as a colleague instead of a student. That's on me."

Clarissa disagreed. "There is no way this is your fault."

"No, *that* part is my fault." He motioned around the clean library. "You staying overnight is *not* my fault. You did that on your own. But it's my fault that I made you think that would be OK." He left the library and walked into the central part of the room. "This is the kind of thing an assistant director would do, should do. I would love an assistant with your organizational skills and your musicianship. And, honestly, your OCD. My room could use some OCD."

He sat down on the piano bench. "If you *were* my assistant, I would be taking you out for breakfast or something."

"Thank you?" Clarissa wasn't sure what to say.

"But you're not an assistant, no matter how much I may wish or act like you are. I have to figure out what to do."

Students were not supposed to be in the school without a teacher in the room with them. School policy was clear on that. Roberts took a risk every time he left the room during class to talk to someone on the stage. He suspected there was an even more strongly worded policy about spending the night in the building. He kept looking around the library, remembering the stacks of unfiled music that had piled up over the years. *There is no way the four of them could have done this and gotten home at any reasonable hour.*

"I am going to have to think about this. Seriously." He looked around the room. "How many hours did it take the four of you to do this?"

"Twelve."

"Wow. It took four people twelve hours to clean that mess?" He felt somewhat vindicated about feeling so overwhelmed. It was no wonder he'd given up. "So, you spent the night?"

"Not exactly." She looked at Angel. "We were going to, but we got interrupted."

That would certainly change things if they were interrupted. Who interrupted them? "Really? Did anyone see you in here?"

"No. They didn't see us. We heard Coach talking to Coach Davis in the hall after they got back from the game."

"Coach Davis is a good guy." Roberts wished he had an assistant like Coach Davis, someone he could talk to who actually understood his job and what he was trying to do. Someone to help with the band, do sectionals, things like that. Help him organize the room.

Clarissa did not want to get into the details of that conversation. "Anyway, we went home after that and came back up the next morning. The building was open for some basketball thing."

"And you propped the door open when you left Friday night, I'm guessing."

"Yes."

Roberts looked at Angel. "Just to be clear, this does not mean that your community service is finished. That is based on time served, not on whether the job is finished. You still have whatever's left of your ninety hours" He looked around the band room. "I'm going to have to find something else for you to do in here." He missed the old days of chalkboards when you could just send a kid outside to beat erasers on the sidewalk. "We'll have to figure that out when you come in this afternoon."

Clarissa nodded towards Angel. "He worked hard. I kept track of his time. He did twelve hours, just like the rest of us."

"That's one more thing I'm going to have to think about, whether he can even count those hours since I wasn't here." Bending school rules was bad enough. He wasn't sure if he wanted to test the patience of the court.

It was getting close to time for the first bell. "I'll think about this today. Let's talk about it after school." He walked Clarissa and Angel to the door. "And tell Hashim and Skyler I want to talk to them after school. And both of you."

31

Getting Real, Real Fast

Compartmentalization is a survival skill for any teacher, but especially for a teacher that sees the same students multiple times in one day. Clarissa was in the band room for three hours in the afternoon. All of the jazz band members were there at least twice, fourth hour for concert band and sixth hour for jazz. Roberts remembered one year when he had the same student in five different classes: rock band, guitar, choir, concert band, and jazz band. And it wasn't even a student that he particularly liked to be around. To stay sane, Roberts had learned to compartmentalize his life. He learned to reboot his brain after every hour when it came to how he looked at his students.

Any disagreement or problem he might have with a student in first hour was forgotten when the student came back later in the day, even if it was the very next hour. As far as Roberts was concerned, they were two different students, one in first hour, the other in second. It wasn't always easy, especially at first, but it proved to be the only way Roberts could get through his day. Otherwise, he would just stay angry. That's no way to live. When Roberts said, "We'll talk about this after school," he meant after school and not in another class later in the day.

Skyler and Hashim walked into the band room as the first-hour rock band was wrapping up. Skyler listened to the drummer but offered no critique. Hashim did not seem to enjoy watching another student playing the Fender bass. "It's like watching someone else while they dance with your crush."

"I'm sure the bass loves you more," Skyler said.

Roberts walked over to them. "You're early." Really early. Concert band wasn't until fourth hour, right after lunch.

"Just thought we'd check out the rock band. They're not bad, especially for only three weeks."

"Right. I forgot that you two were such rock band groupies." Roberts nodded his head to the music. "Well, Louie, Louie sounds like a drunken frat party, so I guess they're on track for greatness." He listened a few more seconds, then spoke to Skyler and Hashim.

"Did Clarissa talk to you?"

The drummer and her bass player nodded.

"So we're good for after school today?"

Hashim spoke up. "Yes." Skyler was more hesitant. "I may have to find a way home."

Roberts looked at her. "Be here. Find a way to make that happen. Are we clear on that?"

"Yes."

And that was it. Nothing else was said about the library or the weekend for the rest of the day. Hashim and Skyler stayed until the bell rang and then went to their second-hour classes. They saw Clarissa in the hall.

"Why didn't he say anything?" As a ninth-grader, Skyler had the least experience in dealing with Roberts, especially when he was angry or had a lot on his mind. She didn't think she'd seen him angry yet.

Clarissa and Hashim looked at each other. "Don't worry," Clarissa said. "He will." Hashim agreed. "You do not want to miss that meeting after school today."

"If you need a ride, I'll take you home," Clarissa offered. "But, you seriously need to be there."

Roberts liked to compartmentalize his day, but he knew he would have to revisit this during his planning period third hour. He knew he would have to talk to Mr. Garcia.

"Got a minute?" It's funny how, even as an adult, there is still a certain pucker factor that comes when you have to visit the principal's office. Just thinking of that term – "pucker factor," not "principal's office" – made Roberts smile. "Pucker factor" was how he and his son rated roller coasters, especially that first big climb when everything inside you tightens up with each ratcheting click.

Mr. Garcia pointed to a chair and closed his computer. "What's up?"

"I have a situation." Roberts told Garcia what had happened, including how he felt responsible for blurring the line between student and colleague with Clarissa.

"Well," the booming voice was not just for the microphone. "That sometimes happens, especially with those gifted and talented students like her. She's going to major in music, right?"

"Music Education. Yes."

Mr. Garcia leaned angrily across his desk. "You're not dating her, are you?"

"Oh, God, no. No." Roberts was shocked by the implication. "Nothing like that. I just think of her as an assistant director sometimes instead of a student. She's a great kid."

The Principal pushed back his chair. "So, this great kid decided to spend the night in the school with three of her friends? One of whom is not such a great kid. Isn't Angel doing community service in the band room?"

"Yes. That was why Clarissa and the others were there." Roberts laughed a little. "Clarissa, Hashim, and Skyler. They've started calling themselves The Trio because of jazz band. Piano, bass, drums. It's a rhythm section thing." He smiled, thinking about how well jazz band was going this year. "They are amazing."

Garcia held up his hand before Roberts went completely off on a tangent. "I'm sure they are. What do you want to do about this?"

Roberts sat back in his chair. "Clarissa is a lot like the managers that the Coaches for their teams."

"Yes."

"And I know that at least one of those managers... I think his name is José... has a key."

"Yes, he does. The coaches kept giving their keys to him because he needed to do things in the building. It was easier just to issue a key to him." It was Mr. Garcia's turn to lean forward. "But that is not public information. That is an exception to school policy for one particular case."

"Clarissa plays that same role in the band room. I trust her completely. She can run a rehearsal. She's helped manage our fundraisers. I rely on her just like Coach relies on José."

"So, you think she needs a key?"

"No. I am not asking for that. That would be seen as a reward in this case. I don't want to reward this. But I do think that we should take her history into consideration. It's not like they vandalized the school or had some big party in the band room. You should see the library. They spent 12 hours working in there. They didn't have time to mess around and still do all that work."

"I see." Garcia had given up on getting Roberts to organize or even straighten up the library. Roberts was a great teacher. His kids loved him. But he struggled with organizational skills. Garcia recognized Roberts as what happens when a boy with ADD grows up. Roberts had never mentioned his ADD to Garcia, but the signs were apparent to anyone with any experience in a classroom.

Garcia repeated his question. "So, what do you want to do about this?"

"I was thinking two weeks detention, served in the band room after school."

207

"And?" Garcia wasn't going to let them or Roberts off that easy. "What else?"

Roberts threw himself on the mercy of the court, or, in this case, the Principal. "What would you recommend?"

"They will not perform at this week's game. They are ineligible." Mr. Garcia could recite the rule from the student handbook by memory. "Students who are in detention for any reason are automatically ineligible to participate in extracurricular activities for the duration of that detention."

Roberts wanted to argue that band students received a grade for playing at the games and it was therefore not extracurricular, but he knew better. All of them, including Roberts, were getting off pretty easy, all things considered. If Garcia wanted to, he could have made this much worse.

"One more thing." Mr. Garcia spoke just as Roberts reached for the doorknob. "This was a court ordered community service. I can't tell you what to do with that. It's ultimately up to you. But I would *strongly* recommend that you not sign a timecard for any work that happened while you were not in that room."

"Understood."

The rest of the day went along like any other. The Trio Plus One ate lunch together, opting to eat at school instead of going off-campus. Compartmentalized or not, they did not want to risk being late for concert band today.

Roberts was his usual self during concert band, even when he was talking directly to Hashim about how to play an uncommon rhythm or helping Skyler tune that timpani with the really touchy pedal. He said nothing about the library, the weekend, or anything until the bell rang and The Trio was about to walk out the door.

"So, we're all good for this afternoon?" He got three very humble yeses for a response.

"Good. Be sure and tell Angel that I am looking forward to seeing him."

Like Skyler, Angel was unfamiliar with Roberts' way of dividing his day into individual units. He had been dreading the walk to weights class all day, not because he would have to deal with Coach again, but because he did not want to walk by the band room. Roberts always stood outside his door, greeting students as they walked into his room and saying hello to students who were on their way to another class. Angel knew that Roberts would be waiting for him.

He tried to sneak by, but it's hard to hide in the hall.

"Hey Angel," Roberts called as he approached the room. Then he stepped out into the hall so Angel would either have to stop or do some awkward maneuver to get around him.

"We still good for this afternoon?" His voice was friendly. If Angel hadn't known any better, he would have thought they were going to watch a ballgame or something.

"We're good."

And that was it.

He saw Skyler and Hashim in weights. "Roberts seems OK with this."

Hashim did not share Angel's confidence. "He's like that. I've seen him rip a kid apart in one hour and then act like nothing happened when he has that kid in class the next hour."

Coach seemed more surly than usual today, but he still did not say anything to Angel. Coach's mood was often reflected in his musical choices for the day. Today was an '80s Metal Band day. Those used to be Angel's favorite days. Today, it just seemed loud. Skyler was doing the bench press but with the bar only, no additional weights. With no help coming from Coach, Angel had stepped in and had shown Skyler different lifts for developing different muscle groups.

Mr. Garcia and his booming voice came in about twenty minutes into class. He walked in, looked at Coach, then went straight to the speakers. He turned off the sound before he said anything. Not that he needed the sound turned off. Mr. Garcia's voice could easily overpower most sound systems. The room got very quiet.

Mr. Garcia glanced at Coach. Then he looked around the room.

"Skyler." There was a pause that was either for dramatic effect, reverberation, or just out of habit. Angel could not tell which, but no hacking like when he spoke on the intercom. Hashim especially appreciated the lack of the hack.

"I need you to come with me." Then he turned to Coach. "Coach. You may turn your music up now."

Hashim walked over to Angel as soon as the ear-damaging volume had been restored.

"Is he going to call each one of us down there one at a time?"

Angel shook his head. "I don't think so. He would have just used the microphone for that. I don't think this has anything to do with this weekend." Angel might not have known what was going on, but he had a good idea. Garcia may have come for Skyler, but the Principal was sending a very clear message to Coach. "Something else is going on."

They finished up weights. Skyler was still in the office, so Hashim walked into the band room for jazz band alone.

Roberts noted the absence of Hashim's partner in crime. "Where's Skyler?"

"Mr. Garcia came in weights and said he wanted to talk to her."

Jerry put his mouthpiece in his trumpet, mindlessly slamming it into the receiver and probably getting it stuck in the process, which meant that Roberts would have to fix it later. "Does this mean you're going to play drums today?"

Then, as if on cue, Skyler entered the room to an eruption of cheers and adulation. She smiled, waved like a rock star, and took her rightful seat on the drum throne.

Hashim walked past her as he went to his seat. "What's going on? Are we in trouble?"

Skyler twirled a drumstick in each hand.

"Coach," she mouthed silently. Then she smiled and said, in a very loud voice, "Let's play!"

Rehearsal went well. Angel arrived in the band room at the same time he had been showing up for the past three weeks. The Trio was conferring in the corner when he came in. Roberts, Angel, and The Trio went to the stage. For the first time since that morning, Roberts brought up what Angel was now referring to as "the Second Incident."

"First, let me say how grateful I am that you cleaned up the library. Your heart was in the right place, even if your brain was not fully engaged." He looked at Clarissa. "What were you thinking?"

She started to say something, but Roberts interrupted. "Don't. That was a rhetorical question."

"Secondly, we would not be having this conversation if you guys had just told me what was going on. I could have stayed here, and none of this would be a problem. You took a huge risk by doing that. And it was a risk you didn't have to take."

He looked at Angel. "I hope you appreciate the friends you've made here."

Angel looked at Skyler and Hashim, then at Clarissa, who was standing beside him. "I do."

Roberts looked very serious. "Was there *anything* else that went on that night that I need to know about? Did you go into any other rooms? Did you see anyone? I need to know everything that happened that night."

Clarissa reprised her role as the spokesperson for the group. "Nothing else happened. No one saw us. We overheard Coach talking to Coach Davis, but they didn't know we were here."

"And you're sure about that?"

"Absolutely."

"Here's what we're going to do. Each of you will have detention after school for thirty minutes for the next ten days. You will serve that detention in the band room. You may practice during that time."

Clarissa seemed skeptical. "So basically, we show up and practice?"

"Yes."

"Just like we already do? Actually, I usually stay for an hour, so half of what I already do?"

"Yes. Skyler that goes for you and Hashim too. Show up, practice for thirty minutes for the next ten days, and we'll call it good."

Clarissa was very grateful. The others were still trying to figure out what just happened.

"There is one more thing. Mr. Garcia thinks you should not play with the band at Friday's game. You are officially ineligible for this week."

Roberts could tell that The Trio had not expected that. "But the drums..." Skyler said.

"We got by without you last year. We can get by on Friday. Sorry, Skyler. You will be missed, I assure you. But no one is irreplaceable. Not even me. And I would prefer not to be replaced at this time."

"Hashim, same with you. I'll be playing bass at the game."

Roberts turned to Angel. "I still don't know what to do with you. You'll also be on detention, but you can do that while you're working, just like they're going to do theirs while they practice. It's the court stuff that's the problem. I'll have to figure that out." He looked at the four of them. "This could have gone very badly. If the alarms had gone off and the police had shown up, that could have gone real wrong real fast."

"You're just lucky it didn't."

32

Stepping Up

The detentions that really weren't detentions began forthwith. Roberts decided that Angel's new job would be guitar tech. He would replace strings, tune the guitars, and polish them up until they shined. That would be ongoing. Strings break all the time. He could work in the percussion closet when the guitars didn't need his attention, although it did not sound like that would happen very often. "If you play guitar for fifty years," Roberts told Angel, "you will spend 25 years tuning your guitar and 25 years playing on a guitar that's out of tune." Roberts said Angel would be the first person to learn how to tune a guitar before he learned how to play one. Angel was fine with that. Anything was better than the library.

Angel couldn't hear a guitar well enough to tune it with all the sound in the band room, so Roberts took him to the stage. They could still hear the band kids practicing, but they could at least hear the guitars they were working on. Roberts let Angel use an electronic tuner even though he firmly believed that a guitar player should be able to tune his instrument by ear. He refused to give up yet another skill to electronics.

Clarissa decided to spend the first 30 minutes, the official "detention minutes," of her usual hour of practice time working on piano instead of clarinet. She was enjoying the piano more each day. She still loved clarinet – she understood that clarinet was her ticket to college – but being part of The Trio made her want to get better at the piano, if for no other reason than to stay ahead of the freshman and sophomore that were sure to challenge her for the Best Saint Musician award at the award banquet at the end of the year.

"They can have their turns after I graduate," she thought. *"But not when I'm still here."*

At 5:30, everyone packed up to go home. Angel was actually looking forward to seeing his mother after having not seen her since Friday morning. *This is some high hope, low expectation stuff right here.*

His low expectations proved to be correct. Mom was not home. There was no sign she had been home. He sent a text

Where are you?

which he quickly followed with another text

Are you OK?

He knew better than to expect an immediate response, just like he knew better than to call. Even under the best of circumstances, texting or calling his mom was more like putting in a request for an appointment than it was any real form of communication.

He hoped that Clarissa would be more immediate with her response.

Angel: What to get something to eat?

"Mom? I'm going to go grab something with Angel. OK?

216

Clarissa: *Maybe. More fish tacos?*

Angel: *I was thinking more Thai.*

Clarissa: *That works. Be there in a few.*

"So, Mom? OK? See ya'.'"

Angel meant to ask her if she wanted him to pick her up, but apparently, that would not be necessary. She was a strong independent woman.

Over dinner, Angel told her that he had not seen his mother since Friday morning.

Clarissa put down her chopsticks. "Sounds like this is more than a sleepover."

"Yeah. Much more than a sleepover." Angel didn't say it, but he suspected she hadn't been to work either. He thought about calling her office tomorrow and asking to speak to her. Nobody there would recognize his voice. That might work.

The server brought the check. Angel pulled out the credit card to pay.

Clarissa noticed there were two names on the card. "Wait. Do you share that card with your mom?"

"Yes." He held up the card. That was a little embarrassing, getting caught using your mom's credit card. So much for being the strong independent man.

"That's the same card my parents let me use." Her eyes lit up. "You know you could use that card to see where she's been. Maybe. If she's been using it."

"What do you mean?"

"Don't you ever pay bills? I use their app to pay my credit card bill. See?" Clarissa held up her phone so Angel could see the app. Angel had to admit that his only interaction with the credit card had been to buy things. He was not involved in the "paying the bills" portion of the credit industry. Another embarrassing truth of his life exposed.

Clarissa looked like a TV detective excited about a new mystery. "Just go to the website and look at the transactions." She remembered who she was talking to. "You do know how to get into the website, right?"

"Yes. I've used it to see how much money was on the card." He could at least do *that* much.

"So you know the password and how to do that. I can help."

"I don't have that app on my phone. All of that stuff is on her computer at the house."

"I can still help."

Did she just suggest coming over to my house? He smiled. "I would like that."

Clarissa slapped his hand playfully but left her hand resting on his. "We're talking about helping with the card, Angel. Nothing else."

Still, this evening suddenly looked more promising than before. And the credit card was a good idea, too. Clarissa followed Angel to his house. He went to the website to look for recent transactions.

Clarissa seemed very familiar with the process, so Angel let her sit in the chair while he looked over her shoulder. He moved in a little close and noticed the way her hair smelled, but not so close that Clarissa would be uncomfortable. He had actually gotten quite good at this particular move. At least something good was coming out of this.

"Some places don't post payments right away, so these may not be in order. But they should be close. And they should give us some idea about where she might be." She looked at Angel. "She's probably just here in town. She may even be at that guy's house. But, knowing guys, they've probably gone out to eat or bought something somewhere." She looked back at the computer. "I don't picture Boy Toy to be the kind of man who would have a problem with a woman paying for everything."

Angel agreed. "He probably doesn't even have a job."

"What a bum."

"Probably claps on one and three."

Clarissa sat up. "What do you know about clapping on one and three?"

"I heard Skyler say it the other day. I figured it was a band geek insult."

Clarissa shook her head and turned her attention back to the computer. There it was, a screen full of recent transactions. "Looks like they spent Friday night at a hotel in Denver." She looked at Angel. "Did she say anything about going to Denver?"

"No. She said nothing about any of this. I came home Friday night, and she wasn't here." Angel stood up, away from the screen and tried to change the conversation. "It's scary how easy it was to find that."

"Wait." Clarissa spun the chair around. "You knew she was missing Saturday, and you went to file that music anyway?"

"What was I going to do? I wasn't going to just leave it for you guys to figure out. Besides, this is not the first time she's had an unannounced sleepover. It's not like she checks in with me before she does these things. She's just never been gone for more than a couple of days. I thought she'd be home Sunday."

"But she wasn't," Clarissa wondered about the other parts of Angel's life that she didn't know about. "And you went to school today knowing she was gone? How do you do that?"

"I start by waking up. Then I usually have breakfast..."

"No, that's not what I meant. I mean, how do you think about anything at school when this is going on at home?"

"You get used to it. Or you just don't think about anything at all. Honestly, it's not that different when she's here." He thought for a moment and allowed himself a wry smile. "I guess I have low expectations." The smile, small though it might have been, disappeared altogether. "And for that matter, low hope." He really wanted to change the subject.

"What's she doing?" he said.

Clarissa realized Angel probably didn't want to talk about his mom, or at least not about how much he might miss her. "I don't think it would be this easy if you weren't on the same card." She looked at the screen again. She pointed to the screen. "This is where they got gas, a little outside of Denver. Doesn't look like they ate anything that night, but they may not have used a credit card for everything either." She tapped at a transaction on the screen. "But they apparently did go to a liquor store." She looked at Angel with an apologetic face.

"She prefers her calories in liquid form. What else is there?"

"Checked into another hotel. Still in Denver. That's weird."

"They probably checked out of the first hotel thinking they were going to come back here and then decided to stay there instead. Or, they decided they were in no condition to drive and decided to stay there. Give them credit for at least that much intelligence." He unconsciously put his hand on Clarissa's shoulder. "I don't think they have a real strict itinerary."

"They're eating well." Clarissa pointed to a transaction. "There's $179 at Sushi Den."

"She doesn't even like fish."

Clarissa looked over her shoulder at Angel. "She's not the only one on this trip." She wanted to add, *"And she's probably one of those women who say they like something even if they don't,"* but decided against it.

Angel sighed. "True."

"And here's another hotel last night, Sunday night." Clarissa looked at Angel. "Still in Denver. Different hotel. Looks like this one is a definite downgrade from the night before."

"Can you tell me where they are tonight?"

Her finger scrolled down the list of transactions. "No. There's another gas station. That looks like a bar. Both of those are in Denver. Oh!"

"What?" Angel thought she found something.

"I've been to this place. It's a Chinese hot pot place on Colorado Blvd. Either your mom or her boyfriend has really expensive tastes."

"She doesn't, and he isn't."

"They either haven't checked into a hotel for tonight, or the bank hasn't posted the transaction yet." She looked up at Angel. "They may not run it until tomorrow morning after they check out."

She swiveled the chair around to face Angel, who was much closer than she realized. And that was oddly OK. "She may be on her way home."

"Yeah." Angel checked his phone just in case he had missed any messages. Nothing. He noticed the time. It was almost 9:00.

Clarissa didn't know what to do. "I need to get home before my dad gets all like he gets. Call me later?"

"Sure."

Relationships have certain milestones. The first time you meet. The first conversation. The first time somebody helps you out when you are buried so deep, you feel like you'll never get out. The first time somebody's there when you really need somebody there. The first real embrace. Not some shallow hug or some excuse to cop a feel. The first hug that lets you know somebody cares. The first hug that comes when you really need a hug.

This was that First Hug.

33

Are You OK?

For someone who made her living working with people who make bad decisions, Delores had no idea why she kept making so many bad decisions. Maybe she'd been making unwise choices all her life and was only just realizing how those misjudgments were piling up. The part of her brain that went to college knew she was in over her head. The other part of her brain, the part that didn't go to college, told her it didn't matter, that she deserved to give herself a break. After all, she'd been through a lot. The divorce. Being a single Mom for almost two years now. Having a super stressful job with unappreciative, often resentful, angry clients. That part of her brain, the part that didn't go to college and yet still managed to dominate her thoughts, told her she deserved a break. The part of her brain that went to college told her this wasn't the break she needed.

She looked at the texts that her phone said were sent four hours ago.

Angel: *Where are you?*

Angel: *Are you OK?*

It wasn't that she *couldn't* answer Angel's questions. Of course she knew where she was. And answering the second question was as simple as touching the suggested autoreply. "Yes." She just couldn't will herself to do it. She was just too tired. Literally too physically and emotionally drained to lift a finger to click "Yes" to reply to her son. *How sad is that?*

Ending a marriage is easy. You decide it's over then you get a divorce. There might be an argument about who gets the house and your son; maybe a fight over the macaw that he said he never liked, but took anyway. But, emotionally, it's a relatively straightforward process once you accept that your shared life isn't working anymore. Granted, getting to that acceptance is painful enough to make up for any slack at the end. But the grand finale? Not so much. Divorce is just the flatlining of a patient who was already in a coma. You've already said goodbye by then.

Quitting a job is easy. You find a new job, or maybe not, and move on. Or you screw up so much that you get yourself fired. She could think of at least two coworkers who were fired because they quit doing their job long before they planned on leaving Social Services. Delores sipped her drink and wondered how close she was to that kind of exit. She still worked with her clients. And she thought about them a lot on the mornings that she was late. She hadn't quit. She just had late-to-work issues. The only client that was falling through the cracks was her.

Turns out, it's even easy to ignore your son once you decide that he'd be better off without you. She looked at the text again.

Angel: *Where are you?*

Angel: *Are you OK?*

"No, I am not OK," she said to an empty hotel room. Her intern was gone, distracted by another woman he met at a bar last night. She should have seen that one coming. It was the same way he was distracted by her when they first met. He didn't even have the courtesy to give her a ride back home. She barely got her stuff out of his car so she could schlep it all to a hotel. Of course she understood. Of course she was nice about it. "I understand, sure. Don't worry. I'll take the bus. I'll be fine." All she had left were hotel receipts and an empty bottle on the floor beside the couch. And another bottle over there.

So much for her big, spontaneous adventure. She was four hours away from home with no car. Delores was embarrassed, sad, alone. And a lot of other emotions that she didn't feel like sorting through at the moment. The only thing she didn't feel was angry. What would be the point?

At least one of the bottles wasn't empty. And there were more in the lobby just waiting to show up on her bill in the morning. Those decisions were still easy enough to make.

Angel: *Are you OK?*

She wanted to say yes, to tell her only child that his mother was fine, just working some things out. Taking a little break. She loved Angel. It was her life that she just couldn't stand. But answering those questions would lead to other questions, and more questions, and on and on until, eventually, someone would ask her to explain how she reached this point in her life and what she planned to do to work through it. Delores knew that she did not have those answers. Why start the course if you already know you're going to fail the final?

She allowed herself one plaintive sarcastic laugh. "We should have taken my car. Then at least I could have left him and driven myself home." She took another sip. "I'd probably just end up in this same hotel, and he'd be driving away in my car. And I'd be telling him to have a good time and be careful while I waved goodbye and kept on making car payments."

The intern was a charmer, and that charm had cost her a lot of money. Delores felt embarrassed for having been used. She hadn't said much to Angel about the divorce. There was no need for him to know that his father had at least one affair that she knew of, maybe more. But she did remember telling him that old men dated girls because they couldn't handle women. Perhaps her intern charmed vulnerable older women because he couldn't control strong younger women. That, and community college girls don't have the money to underwrite things like spontaneous road trips to Denver for sushi.

I should have stuck with being as spontaneous as a calendar.

It was dark when she dragged her overnight bag into the hotel. The woman at the front desk said her room had a view of the mountains, but in the darkness, she could only see the lights of the city. It was too dark to see the mountains she paid for.

She opened the final unopened bottle. She decided she would figure out how to make the four-hour trip home tomorrow, right after she decided whether she wanted to go anywhere at all.

34

While You Were Sleeping

Clarissa's phone buzzed at 2:48 Monday morning. She would have slept through it had she not fallen asleep with her phone in her hand.

Angel: *She's in the Hyatt in downtown Denver. They just posted it.*

"Has he been checking for that all night?"

Clarissa: *Did she reply yet?*

Angel: *No*

Clarissa sat up and tried to be awake enough to think. If Angel's mom wanted him to know where she was, she would have told him by now. Even if she only wanted to tell him good night, she would have told him that. Basically, if she wanted to talk to him, she would have. Assuming there wasn't any kind of problem, which Clarissa realized was a very large assumption on her part, she had deliberately chosen not to reply. She did not want to talk right now.

On one level, Clarissa could almost understand her need to get away, even if this was not a good way to do it. She could not understand why a mother would not tell her son whether or not she was alright.

She wondered if Angel was thinking these same things or if he was so intent on finding his mother that he was missing the message she was already sending with her non-response. Sometimes people say the most when they don't speak.

Clarissa: *What are you going to do?*

Angel didn't know what he was going to do. He was relieved that she was in a hotel and safe. At least he assumed she was safe. She wasn't in some hospital somewhere, so that was good. Thankfully, there was an autoreply that predicted his inability to make a decision.

Angel: *I don't know.*

"If I leave now, I could be there by seven." He'd driven there before, but never by himself. It was coming up on 3AM, and he hadn't slept since 5:30 yesterday morning. He wasn't sure how long he could stay awake on adrenaline and caffeine.

He checked his messages again just in case she had replied. Nothing.

"She doesn't want me to know where she is." He wondered if he should respect her silent request to be left alone or if he owed it to his mom to ignore it and go to her anyway. He thought about what Roberts had said about staying in a bad relationship until the pain of staying was greater than the fear of leaving. He seemed to have the exact opposite problem. His fear of staying away was rapidly gaining on the potential pain of finding her when she did not want to be found.

His phone buzzed.

Clarissa: *Did you get any sleep at all?*

Clarissa didn't seem to think he should go. He knew she was right, even if he didn't want to admit it. If he left now, he'd just end up sleeping in his car somewhere along the way and arriving at the same time that he would if he stayed home and got some sleep before he left. That was the best-case scenario. The worst possibility would be if he fell asleep on the way. Mom did that once when he was younger. They both woke up as soon as they left the road, but they still ended up in that big grassy space they put between the lanes on I-70. He did not want to do the same.

He sent a text to Clarissa.

Angel: *I'm driving to Denver.*

"That's just dumb," Clarissa said to the stuffed bear that lived on her bed. "Not surprising. But dumb."

Clarissa: *Be careful.*

Angel sat out on his mission to find his mother. He gassed up his car, grabbed something to eat, and was on the road by a little before 3:30.

As predicted, he was sleeping in a gas station parking lot a little more than two hours later.

35

Searching

If you want to sleep late in a parking lot, it's best not to park your car so it faces the eastern horizon, especially if that horizon is on the unobstructed high plains of Colorado. Angel did not want to sleep at all, but he didn't have a choice. Sleep is the strongest of all human drives, stronger than hunger, sex, or anything else. You can force yourself to go without food. Some people go a lifetime without having sex. You can only stay awake for so long before your body says no more. You will eventually sleep.

Angel had not parked facing the open eastern horizon on purpose. He just pulled into the first available space he could find while driving with the mental acuity of someone with a blood-alcohol level of .10, twenty percent higher than the legal limit. He remembered something from driver's ed, about how 24 hours without sleep was the same as having a blood-alcohol level of .10. After that last hour of driving with his eyes half shut and his head bobbing up and down, he believed it. Had he been pulled over for weaving as he tried to stay awake, he would have been suspected of driving while intoxicated and probably would have been asked to say the alphabet backward or dance on one leg while reciting the Pledge of Allegiance in Tagalog, the language of his father.

Or something. Or he could have been accused of being high. Again. At least his urine test would have come back clean. Another successful rehabilitative win for the American criminal justice system. Yeah. Go War On Drugs.

He barely remembered pulling into the parking lot in Limon at all. He was awakened by a blazing sun blasting head on through his windshield with no clouds, trees, or buildings to block the light. This is the more or less flat part of Colorado, the part they don't advertise. It was a glorious morning sunrise, once Angel's eyes and brain adjusted enough to figure out what it was. Thank goodness he would be driving away from it once he got on the road.

He looked at his phone. 7:21. And still no messages from his mother. And he was still two hours from downtown Denver. In another nine minutes, he would be officially late for school. An hour after that and he would have an officially unexcused absence. He texted Clarissa.

Angel: *In Limon. Just woke up.*

"As long as I'm here, I might as well get some gas." Something occurred to him as he filled up his tank. He sent another text to Clarissa.

Angel: *Could you access my credit card on your app?*

Angel could have downloaded the app to his phone and seen the transactions on his own. He justified asking Clarissa by telling himself that he didn't want to have to do that while he was driving. The truth was that he wished she was with him, and this was a way of at least feeling as if she was, kind of. A virtual partner for his emergency road trip.

Clarissa: *I would need your credit card info and your login. Do you trust me with that?*

Trust her? Why wouldn't he trust her? He trusted her more than he trusted his own mother. He laughed. The lack of exaggeration in that cliché at this time in his life was sadly amusing. He sent her the info and got back on the road.

Angel had been back on the road for about half an hour when his phone rang. It was Clarissa.

"Good morning." He tried to smile when he spoke. Someone told him people can hear you smile on the phone. He wanted her to know he was OK without having to say it.

"Hi. I thought I would call so you didn't have to text while you're driving. We can't use her card to track her like that. You saw how long it took for the hotel to post online. It might be hours or even days before we see anything."

Angel had not thought of that, but he assumed she was right. He didn't know when Mom checked in, but he hoped it was before two in the morning when he finally saw the transaction. Although, with her, that was a possibility.

"You're right." He sighed. "Any other ideas."

"Just one."

Delores woke up, remembered where she was, and started trying to think of what to do with her life. That proved to be way too big of a topic for such an early hour. She decided instead to focus on what she would do with her day. That was still too much of a chunk. She settled for weighing the pros and cons of whether she should get out of bed.

233

After some deliberation, she decided to stay in bed and just look out the window. Instead of the promised mountain view, all she could see was the back of a not particularly attractive neighboring hotel. Apparently, one had to get out of bed to actually see the mountains from this room.

She decided the mountains could wait. Just like her, they weren't going anywhere.

She picked up her phone and read the messages again.

Angel: *Where are you?*

Angel: *Are you OK?*

She remembered ignoring those texts last night. More questions, more decisions she did not want to have to think about. At least Angel hadn't blown up her phone with more text messages when she didn't reply. Maybe he'd given up on her too. Her intern clearly had.

Reality rose along with the sun. She knew that eventually, she would have to go home, if for no other reason than to get some clean clothes. She remembered saying something last night about taking a bus, but she really did not want to do that. All that way. All those people. No chance of any detours or turning back if she decided to change course.

"I'm going to need to rent a car." That would mean taking a cab to the airport to pick it up, but that would work. A few clicks on her phone, and she was looking at an assortment of car rental options. She picked the first one on the list and started filling out the convenient online form.

Pickup point: Denver International Airport

Dropoff point:

That might be a problem. The only place that rented cars in Hoag was a gently pre-owned car dealership that rented out the junker used cars that were on the lot to be sold. There was no rental chain. No Hertz or Enterprise waiting to pick her up.

She tried, anyway.

Dropoff point: Hoag, CO

Invalid destination. Try again.

"Invalid is a good word for that." She tried to think of other options, anything that wasn't a bus. She thought about asking Angel to pick her up, but that would be just too humiliating. Besides, he probably hadn't even noticed she was gone. Or didn't care. Or both. She couldn't say she'd blame him.

There was a train, but she would have to get to Pueblo to catch it. That was still two hours away. She might as well take the bus.

She tried to think of options. There was a U-Haul place in Hoag. She could tell them she was moving, rent their smallest truck, and drop it off when she got home. That would cost more than renting a car, but it would get her within walking distance of her house. And it was probably her only real option. She pulled up the website and started filling out the form. There was a pickup point nearby, just a short cab ride away. Destination Hoag was accepted. No problem there.

She filled typed in her credit card number and…

Card declined. Check your card number and try again.

She thought she had typed that in right. She didn't see a problem. Maybe it was that three-digit code that was almost rubbed off and nearly impossible to read. Must have done something wrong somewhere.

Card declined. Contact your bank for details.

Frustrating. She squinted to see the microprinted phone number on her card, tapped in the last four digits of her card number, and prepared to wade through the menu that had undoubtedly been changed. She expected to hear an entirely too long string of prompts telling her what to do next. She did not expect to hear a human voice and a warning that this call may be recorded for training purposes.

"Hello. May I help you?"

Delores tried not to let her frustrations with her card and her life, or, that matter, the entire planet, show in her voice. "I hope so. I just tried to use my card, and it was declined. Is there a problem?"

"I'll be happy to check on that for you." Long pause.

"Ma'am, I'm going to put you on hold. I'll be right back."

Longer pause. Horrible music.

"I apologize for the wait. Ma'am, it looks like that card has been reported as stolen."

"What? This is my card."

"I'm sure it is ma'am." For the first time in her life, Delores wished she was dealing with a machine. At least machines don't sound sarcastic. "These things happen. Unfortunately, I have no way of verifying that this is actually you."

"You have got to be kidding me."

"We take credit card fraud very seriously, ma'am. I assure you I am not kidding. That card has been frozen. Would you like to request a replacement card? I can have that to you in a week to ten days."

Delores was angry. "No, I would not. I would like to request that you allow me to use the credit card I already have. The one that is in my possession."

"Again, I apologize."

Again, I wish you were a machine. Do they train you people to be condescending?

"There is nothing I can do. A hold was placed on this card at 8:48 this morning." There was a pause. "And looking at these transactions, there does appear to be some unusual activity. Did you stay at four different hotels in the same city on four consecutive nights? There are also several liquor stores and bar transactions. Are those yours as well?"

"Yes, but why should I have to explain my life to you?"

"You don't ma'am. Is there anything else I can help you with today?"

"No!" Times like this made Delores miss the old days of heavy landline phones that you could slam down to hang up on someone. Pounding the little red End Call button on her phone's screen just wasn't the same. Not satisfying at all. Throwing the phone at the wall across the room felt better, though still not as gratifying as knowing the other person was clutching their ear in pain from you dramatically slamming the phone down on them.

It did not occur to her that Angel would report her credit card stolen. It would never have occurred to her that Clarissa was the one who actually did it. She assumed it was what the woman on the phone said. The card was suspended because of what appeared to be unusual activity. "Of course there's unusual activity!" she screamed at the back of the hotel that she could see from her window. "My life is a disaster! There's going to be unusual activity!"

"How bad does your life have to be for a credit card company to question your life choices?"

36

That Same Morning

Angel assumed that checkout time at the hotel was probably 11:00. That seemed to be what he remembered from the few nights he had spent in hotels. He was glad he woke up when he did. He was also glad he had filled up his tank even though it was only half empty at the time. With the credit card canceled, he wouldn't be able to get any gas. He thought he could make it to Denver and then back on what was in the tank now, but he wasn't one hundred percent sure. Good thing the drive home was downhill.

The drive from Limon to Denver isn't nearly as desolate as the drive from Hoag to Limon, but it's still not a very scenic route. Angel kept thinking about the experiences, circumstances, and attitudes that led his mother to do this, the causes and conditions of what was going on. If this was the best she could do, he did not want to know what could be the worst. He thought about last year's psych class and realized he'd been through the entire Kübler-Ross grieving cycle in a single 24 hour period. Denying there was a problem. Angry that the problem exists. He bargained that he could make the drive to Denver without falling asleep. Oh well. You can't win every time. For that matter, he was bargaining right now with his credit card, telling himself that if it meant getting to his mom, he would risk running out of gas. *Let's hope this bet turns out better.* There was the depression of realizing what was going on and, finally, accepting the fact that his mother needed help. He was her son. Mom needed help.

This wasn't the best thing that could have happened, but he understood and accepted that it was the best she could do, given her state of mind, the circumstances, and everything that led up to this moment. Things might have been different if any of those elements had changed along the way, but this is how it is now. If he wanted her to let him take her home, he knew he would have to be willing to accept her as she is without judging what she had done. It really didn't matter how she got here. This is where she is now.

He knew she was hurting. He just hoped she wasn't physically hurt as well.

Traffic was horrible coming into Denver. Colorado has two seasons, its unpredictable winters and its all too predictable Road Construction Season. This was not winter. The lanes that weren't blocked were backed up all along the parking lot formerly known as I-70. He took the first exit he saw that he thought might take him downtown and to the hotel. No sense in burning gas idling on the Interstate.

He drove by the hotel at 10:51. With no card for hotel parking, he decided to take his chances and not pay the parking meter on the street. After circling the block like an airplane with nowhere to land, he ended up parking about six blocks away. He ran to the hotel.

He asked the front desk for the number of his mother's room.

"Sir, I cannot give out guest room numbers. I'm sorry."

"Look." He pulled out his driver's license. "I'm her son. She is not well. I'm here to pick her up."

"It's 11:05. Check out was at 11:00. Are you sure she's still here?"

"Yes! But she won't be if you don't let me get to her."

"I'll call housekeeping."

"Thank you!" Angel watched as the woman called housekeeping. He tried to overhear the room number so he could go up, but the woman at the front desk was too smart for that. Probably had a Master's degree in something but had to take a job at a hotel front desk. Just his luck. A front desk savant.

"Housekeeping will check on her, sir. Please have a seat over there."

Angel took a seat. Hotel lobbies are strange places. Comfortable without being comforting, a fitting atmosphere for a business that pretends to be at home.

He waited. The woman at the desk talked into a radio. Then she looked at him.

He waited some more.

After some time, a long time, his phone buzzed. *Probably Clarissa.*

It wasn't.

Mom: *I'll be down in a few minutes.*

He put the phone down and finally sank into the overstuffed chair in the lobby. He had just closed his eyes when he heard the phone buzz again.

Mom: *Thank you. I love you.*

He texted Clarissa.

Made it.

Then he waited.

And waited.

Angel went to the woman behind the front desk. "My mother said she would be right down. That was 15 minutes ago."

The woman picked up the phone. "Security. I need you in the lobby."

Angel was about to explode. He didn't need security. He needed to check on Mom. He was about to express exactly how strong that need was to the woman when security arrived.

She pointed to Angel. "Please take him to room 730."

Seven floors take forever when you believe your mother is dying. Angel and the security guard ran to the room as soon as the elevator doors opened wide enough for Angel to squeeze through.

He pounded on the door, but there was no answer. "Mom? Mom?" Angel looked at the guard. "We're coming in."

The guard slowly opened the door, unsure of what he might find inside. He expected Angel to run inside the room, but he didn't. The young man stood in the doorway, taking in the room, trying to understand what he was seeing. Delores was sitting on the bed, facing the window with her back to the door, still wearing the clothes that Angel could only assume she had worn the night before, the clothes she had slept in. Her hair was a mess.

The security guard stayed back while Angel went to his mother and sat beside her on the bed. Delores did not look well. Her vacant eyes stared straight ahead. She wasn't drunk, but she wasn't there either.

"They said you could see the mountains," she said. Angel looked out the window. The room was even with the top of the neighboring building. It must have been the lowest floor that could claim to have a view. Barely.

"I just wanted to see the mountains."

Angel looked back at the guard who was waiting a respectful distance outside the door.

"Mom, I bet if we stood up, we could see the mountains." He helped Delores to her feet. "See? There they are. Right there."

"Thank you, Angel." She turned to her son. "Please take me home."

Delores slept most of the way home. Angel was exhausted, but managed to make it back without having to stop and sleep. He went to bed as soon as they got home, grateful that his car lied to him when it said the gas tank was empty. He reminded himself to call the credit card company and tell them he'd found his card.

Angel woke up around 11:00 that night. Mom was sitting on the couch, wearing sweats and reading a book. She didn't look like she was going anywhere. There were no glasses, cups, or bottles in sight. Angel knew that didn't necessarily mean anything, but it seemed like a good sign. She looked sober. Her eyes had some life in them, but Angel could see that she was exhausted.

He told her goodnight and went back to bed.

The next morning she was sitting at the table drinking her coffee, scrolling through her phone.

"Let's go to the Thai place for lunch," Angel offered. He'd been eating there a lot lately, but he thought having lunch with her would be a good way to check up on her to make sure she was OK.

She looked at him and motioned for him to sit down. "I've been thinking." She reached across the table and took both of his hands in hers. "What would I say to me if I was my client?"

"And? What would you say?"

"I would refer me to an addiction counselor." She inhaled deeply. "And I would tell me that it was a good thing that I came in voluntarily instead of having to go through court-ordered rehab for a DUI. Or worse."

"What would you tell you to expect?" Angel was having a hard time keeping up with the pronouns, but the mental challenge made it easier to have this conversation without crying.

"From the counselor? I'm not sure, but I would tell me to listen to what she said, to not argue or think that I know better, and to be ready to do some hard work."

"Is that what you tell your clients?"

She looked at Angel. "Yes." She turned and looked out the window.

Silence.

"My job does have some benefits." She faced Angel. "I called one of our addiction counselors after we got home." She held her son's hands in hers. "She's going to see me today at 9:00. She may want me to check in. I'll let you know."

Angel looked at the time. School could wait.

"I'll take you."

37

Losing It

Angel thought about going home after his mother was checked in and safe. He looked at his phone. If he hurried, he could make it back just at the end of lunch. He pulled into the parking lot and headed towards the front doors.

Clarissa was sitting on a bench in front of the school.

"Welcome back!" Clarissa hugged Angel, then pulled away.

"So, is she OK?"

"I don't know. I hope so." He did that short, exhaling laugh that he did. "High hope, optimistic expectations?"

"Sounds about right."

"She saw one of the addiction counselors where she works. They got her set up in rehab."

"How long will she be there?"

"At least a week, maybe more. We'll see. She'll stay until she's better." He paused. "She checked in voluntarily, so I guess she can leave whenever she wants. I'm just hoping she can stay for as long as it takes." Angel looked at Clarissa as he held the school door open for her. "She's just doing the best she can."

Clarissa stopped before she entered the building. "I am very proud of you."

"For holding the door open? Not that big of a deal." He opened and closed the door a few times while Clarissa looked at him.

"No, silly. For being a good man."

They walked towards the band room for Clarissa's next class. "I told Roberts why you missed detention yesterday, sort of. I told him your Mom was stuck in Denver, and you had to pick her up. I hope that wasn't too much."

"No, that's fine."

"He also said he hopes everything is OK."

"Tell him thanks."

Hashim and Skyler were standing outside the band room. Hashim seemed especially excited to see him.

"You would not believe weights yesterday. I don't know what's going on, but Coach was not happy. Something must be about to happen. You can tell."

"Who knows what's going on with him." Angel really did not care. There were more important things on his mind than Coach. "Maybe he washed that stupid red baseball cap he's been wearing, and it turned all his white sheets pink."

"And what's wrong with pink?"

"Nothing, Skyler. But I'm guessing you won't catch Coach wearing it."

Angel saw Roberts in the hall later when he was on his way to weights.

"Good to see you. Clarissa told me you had to go pick up your mom. Is she OK?"

"She will be. Thanks."

Angel knew something was wrong when he walked into the weight room. He told himself that he was just thinking about what Hashim said earlier. That's why it felt that way. Places don't retain feelings. But something was there, like the feeling in the air before a thunderstorm. He'd heard that your hair stands upright before a lightning strike, that the electricity is already in the air before the lightning bolt forms and hits you. It was that kind of a feeling. Somebody was about to get hit.

Hashim was right. Coach did not look happy.

Coach stood up behind his desk before the bell to start class even finished. He slammed a book down on the desktop to make sure he had everyone's attention. "Listen up, everybody." He was trying to sound like Mr. Garcia, but he didn't have the voice. What he lacked in depth, he tried to make up for with volume. "I am tired of watching you people goof off, make excuses, and otherwise not taking this class seriously." He pounded a fist on his desk to emphasize his words. "You *will* respect this class, you *will* respect this equipment, and, by God, you *better believe* you will respect me! Now, get to work."

Angel, Skyler, and Hashim recognized the tone. It was the same angry voice they heard in the hallway that night.

Skyler got on the bench press and began lifting with ten-pound plates. That was twenty pounds more than the empty bar she lifted all last week. Angel had shown her how to lift so she wouldn't have quite the same risk of crashing the bar on her chest. She was beginning to think she might actually enjoy weights, so long as she could do the exercises that didn't make her biceps and shoulders get too big. She was ending her first set of five reps when Coach walked over to the bench.

"Put more weight on there, *son.*"

Skyler sat up on the bench. "My name is Skyler. You can call me Skyler."

"I know what your name is. Now put some more weight on that bar, *Skyler.*"

Angel was tired and raw. Without thinking, he vented that frustration on Coach.

"She's trying. Give her a break."

Coach stopped in his tracks in the middle of the room. "What did you say to me?"

Hashim stepped up beside Angel and looked at Coach. "He said, 'She's trying. Give her a break.'" Skyler stood up beside her friends.

"I am *done* giving you people breaks!" Coach walked to the speakers, turned off the music, and raised his voice another notch. "Did you hear me? I am *tired* of all of this! All of this!" He stepped towards Angel. "I am done with people making excuses, people getting away with stuff, and pretending that all of this," he raised his hands to face level and waved them around the room, "is normal."

Hashim sensed an impending crescendo. He looked at Angel and slowly made his way towards the door.

Coach was raging. "I am being told what matters, which *lives* matter and which lives do not, by people who honestly do not matter at all. Am I making myself clear?"

"Crystal," said Hashim.

Coach picked up a softball that was on his desk and hurled it at the mirror on the wall opposite the door as if he was a major league pitcher. "This is *not* normal. This is *not* acceptable."

Angel watched as Hashim slowly moved his hand up the wall. Angel could see what Hashim was reaching for. He just had to make sure Coach didn't see it.

"What's not normal is a teacher who hates his students," Angel said. That seemed to get his attention. Coach was no longer looking at Hashim.

Hashim made his move.

One ping in the office meant a teacher was calling on the intercom. A voice came over the speaker. "Coach? Did you call the office?" There was no reply, but there was a lot to hear.

Coach roared. "I am so tired of all the politically correct nonsense that goes on around here, from the front office on down." He threw a tape dispenser across the room. "Nothing but excuses. What this school needs, what this *country* needs, is discipline and respect! And a little gratitude. People need to know who's in charge. People need to know their place."

Skinny Boy made the mistake of a stifled giggle.

"You think this is funny?" Coach picked up an empty barbell and thrashed it around, almost hitting the skinny kid. "This is not funny. This is pathetic." He made a slow circle, wielding the barbell like a club. "*You* are a loser. You are *all* losers. Every one of you." He pointed the barbell at Angel. "Especially you, Loser. Hanging out with your new band geek buddies." The barbell made a loud, hammering sound as Coach slammed it against the frame of the squat rack. The hit seemed to make his voice even louder. "I thought you were a man, Angel. I guess I was wrong." He slowly rotated and looked at almost everyone in the room. "I was wrong about all of you. I was wrong about this entire, pathetic school."

The lights in the room flashed off and then back on. Twice. Angel looked towards the door. Mr. Garcia was standing at the light switch. "Coach, come with me. Coach Davis will cover your class for you. You'll need to bring your keys and anything else you might need with you."

Coach looked at Angel in front of him. Then he turned to see Hashim still standing near the intercom button on the wall.

Mr. Garcia took another step into the room, followed by Coach Davis. His deep voice had the same dramatic pauses that he used when he was on the microphone. "Now, Coach. Let's go." Mr. Garcia gripped Coach's arm and walked him down the hall.

You hear thunder before you see the lightning. But that doesn't mean the lightning isn't there.

Angel walked over to Coach Davis. "Did what I think just happened, happen?"

"Teachers are not supposed to talk about other teachers, Angel. You know that." Then he turned towards Angel. "But yeah. It's been coming for a while. This was the end."

Coach Davis looked around the weight room. These were not athletes, but they were not bad people. They were just regular students who were doing the best they could do. "OK. Everybody get to work."

Coach Davis sat down behind the desk. "Angel. Come here."

Angel put barbell on the squat rack and went over to the desk.

Coach Davis nodded his head towards a chair that was near the desk. "Have a seat." He took a deep breath. "None of this is official, yet, but it looks like I'll be coaching for a while. Maybe the rest of the season. It would be great if our starting running back could be there."

"I have to work after school. It's a court thing."

"I know. Why don't you ask Mr. Roberts if you can switch that so you're working before school. He's usually here when we're lifting at 6:30. I'll talk to him if you need me to. But he'll be doing us a favor, so we can't really push it. Still, I think he might help us out." Coach Davis paused. "Interesting guy, Mr. Roberts. I like him."

"Yeah. I do, too." Angel had high hopes and reasonably high expectations that Roberts would be OK with this, even if he didn't feel comfortable signing off on the hours that Angel and The Trio had worked over the weekend. Angel understood why Roberts felt that way, even if he wished things were different. At least the library was finished and he could spend the rest of the time somewhere else.

"So, can you come in that early? I mean, if that works for Roberts?"

Angel smiled. "I can. I'll see if that works for him." As Angel walked away, he turned back to face Coach Davis.

"Thanks, Coach."

Epilogue

Four Years Later

Schools feel different in the summer. There are no students, which automatically makes a huge difference. Schools shouldn't be that quiet. Desks and chairs are in the halls while rooms are being cleaned. Panels are missing from the ceiling while workers fix wiring and ventilation problems. The front office is the only part of the building that looks anything like it does during the school year, and even that still seems different.

Nothing is permanent.

Mr. Garcia showed Hoag High School's newest assistant football coach to the weight room, then handed him the keys. "And this is where you will spend most of your time. You and Coach Davis will work out a schedule for after school and before school lifting for athletes. You'll be doing weight training classes in here and PE across the hall in the gym. Welcome back to Hoag High School." Mr. Garcia shook his hand. "We are glad you decided to become a Saint!"

The new assistant coach stood alone in his weight room. His classroom. His new home. He thought about the legacy of this place. The strength of it. He was happy to be a part of all of that. He thought about the experiences, circumstances, and attitudes that brought him to this moment. He wondered if he would be standing here if any of those things had been different.

As he was leaving, he stopped by the room next door. Someone was playing the piano. He didn't want to interrupt, so he stopped just outside to listen.

The piano stopped. The new band director saw him at the door. She stood up behind the piano. "Hi! I can't believe it! I heard they had hired a new assistant coach. Is that you?"

"It is." Angel smiled. "Thai or Mexican?"

"Cocina Veracruz."

About the Author

Bob **Seay** teaches high school band and choir in Colorado. An outspoken advocate for social justice, Bob ran for Congress in 2016. In 2013, he wrote 'I Am Not Trayvon Martin." The piece went viral and is considered one of the most important commentaries on the Trayvon Martin case. He writes about politics and social injustice on his blog at bobseay.com. He is also an advocate for mental health, special education, and for people with ADHD.